Praise for
Santiago's Road Home

★ "With every chapter, readers will be further immersed in Santiago's story as they root for his triumph over injustice."
—*Booklist* (starred review)

★ "With unflinching conviction, Diaz sketches a frank, brief account of refugee youth in an uncaring bureaucratic system." —*Kirkus Reviews* (starred review)

"Harrowing but deeply illuminating."
—*School Library Journal*

★ "Diaz's crucial narrative shines a disconcerting light on the plight of children in US detention centers along the southern border." —*Publishers Weekly* (starred review)

SANTIAGO'S
ROAD
HOME

Alexandra Diaz

A Paula Wiseman Book

Simon & Schuster Books for Young Readers

NEW YORK   LONDON   TORONTO   SYDNEY   NEW DELHI

The publisher and the author gratefully acknowledge
Grace Gómez Molinaro, Esq., for her expert review of this book.

SIMON & SCHUSTER BOOKS FOR YOUNG READERS
An imprint of Simon & Schuster Children's Publishing Division
1230 Avenue of the Americas, New York, New York 10020
This book is a work of fiction. Any references to historical events, real people, or real places
are used fictitiously. Other names, characters, places, and events are products of the author's
imagination, and any resemblance to actual events or places or persons, living or dead,
is entirely coincidental.
Text © 2020 by Alexandra Diaz
Cover illustration © 2020 by Beatriz Gutierrez
All rights reserved, including the right of reproduction in whole or in part in any form.
SIMON & SCHUSTER BOOKS FOR YOUNG READERS and related marks are trademarks
of Simon & Schuster, Inc.
For information about special discounts for bulk purchases, please contact Simon & Schuster
Special Sales at 1-866-506-1949 or business@simonandschuster.com.
The Simon & Schuster Speakers Bureau can bring authors to your live event. For more
information or to book an event, contact the Simon & Schuster Speakers Bureau
at 1-866-248-3049 or visit our website at www.simonspeakers.com.
Also available in a Simon & Schuster Books for Young Readers hardcover edition
Book design by Krista Vossen
The text for this book was set in Bembo Std.
Manufactured in the United States of America 0922 OFF
First Simon & Schuster Books for Young Readers paperback edition May 2021
4 6 8 10 9 7 5
The Library of Congress has cataloged the hardcover edition as follows:
Names: Diaz, Alexandra, author.
Title: Santiago's road home / Alexandra Diaz.
Description: First edition. | New York : Simon & Schuster Books for Young Readers, [2020] | "A
Paula Wiseman Book." | Includes bibliographical references. | Audience: Ages 8–12. | Audience:
Grades 4–6. | Summary: Fleeing abusive relatives and extreme poverty in Mexico, young Santiago
endures being detained by ICE while crossing the border into the United States.
Identifiers: LCCN 2019028342 (print) | LCCN 2019028343 (ebook) |
ISBN 9781534446236 (hardback) | ISBN 9781534446243 (pbk) | ISBN 9781534446250 (ebook)
Subjects: CYAC: Refugees—Fiction. | Detention of persons—Fiction. |
Emigration and immigration—Fiction. | Mexicans—United States—Fiction. |
U.S. Immigration and Customs Enforcement—Fiction. | Orphans—Fiction.
Classification: LCC PZ7.D5432 San 2020 (print) |
LCC PZ7.D5432 (ebook) | DDC [Fic]—dc23
LC record available at https://lccn.loc.gov/2019028342
LC ebook record available at https://lccn.loc.gov/2019028343

*To all of those who have been separated
from someone you love, this book is for you.*

PROLOGUE

Somewhere, neither here nor there

The bed creaks under Santiago's shivering body. Maybe it's not a bed, but a coffin.

Had he thought about it, he would have preferred to go a different way—saving lost, invisible unicorns or escaping this prison to be free.

But he'd never thought of death that way before.

Especially not of dying here, like this. Lost and alone. At least now he doesn't have to fight. Doesn't have to try so hard. People who die are at peace. He could use some peace.

He hears voices, but it's unclear if they're real or remembered. What is real, anyway?

He can't hold on anymore. As sure as the blinding

light, death sways closer. Santiago knows it has come for him. He takes a deep breath, embracing the white light. Soon it'll all be over.

And I'm not afraid.

They say a person's life flashes by before dying. But it's not his whole life. Just the events that led to this. The important ones, and the ones Santiago would rather forget.

PART 1

CHAPTER 1

Estado de Chihuahua, México

Santiago watched Tío Ysidro walk by him and the three toddlers as if they were nothing more than rocks in the yard. Not that the toddlers even looked up from their mud pies at the arrival of their *papá*. Just as well, or they would have seen an expression like a lightning storm ready to strike on their *papá*'s face.

He jumped to his feet as the front door slammed behind Tío, ready to urge the kids to safety before the storm broke. Except he wasn't quick enough.

"What do you mean you got fired?" Tía Roberta's voice came clearly through the closed door.

"Have I told you the story of the singing *zanate*?" Santiago whispered excitedly as he pointed to a fence post. He whistled at the bird perched on top of the rotting wood, ready to make up a story on the spot. The children—Jesús, Apolo, and Artemisa—who normally loved hearing Santiago's stories, were too interested in their mud projects to pay attention to anything else. Including the shouts from the house. But the mud wasn't enough to keep Santiago from hearing everything.

"I mean, you insulted the boss's wife, and now I'm fired," Tío Ysidro shouted back.

"When have I met your boss's wife?"

The *viejita* from next door opened her window a bit wider. Since she did not have a TV, her main source of entertainment was eavesdropping on everyone up and down the *calle*. Santiago would have given anything to be entertained by a TV instead.

"Apparently you met her this morning, while she stood in front of you waiting for the bus."

"*¿Patas flacas?*" Tía retorted. "That was her?"

"*¡Patas flacas!*" Artemisa screeched, as if calling someone "skinny legs" was the funniest insult in the world. For a two-and-a-half-year-old, it probably was.

"You called her that? To her face?" Tío exclaimed.

"She cut in front of me!"

Tío Ysidro let out a string of bad words, which Santiago covered up by splashing his hands in the mud and getting the kids to follow suit.

Still, Tío's next yell remained completely audible. "How could you say that to her?"

A crash like a pot being thrown to the floor erupted from the kitchen. This time, Jesús and Artemisa looked up from the mud.

"Great, that was our dinner." Tía Roberta's accusations came out so loud and clear the *viejita* next door must have been grinning at the great reception. "Unless you want to pick up the rice from the floor, we have nothing else to eat tonight, and we're all going to starve."

"How can there be nothing to eat? I gave you money for groceries two days ago."

"Yeah, and it's gone. You barely gave me enough for one meal."

"Fine. You go look for a job and see how much you earn after working twelve or fifteen hours a day." The door banged open and slammed shut after Tío Ysidro. If Santiago and the toddlers were invisible before, they were nonexistent this time. Tío stepped on a stray shoe one of the kids had taken off and didn't notice it under his foot before he crossed the street in the direction of the local bar.

Santiago waited for Tía to run after her husband, but the door stayed shut.

A stray curl fell over Apolo's eye. Santiago brushed it away, careful not to get mud from his own hands onto the boy's face.

"Too bad these mud pies won't taste as good as they look," he said softly to his charges. "Maybe we'll just need to gobble you guys up instead." He smeared mud on Jesús's bare belly and got a giggle in reply.

Apolo and Artemisa wiggled their hands at Santiago and did the butt-bounce dance. He tickled all three of them until they were pushing themselves up on wobbly feet to run away with shrieks of laughter, only to slip and land back in the mud.

"Why are my children playing in the mud like some *huérfanos*?" Tía Roberta stood in front of them with her hands on her hips and a scowl across her red face.

Santiago ignored the orphan comment, like he did most of the insults his *tía* sent his way. Sure, the kids were dirty, covered from head to diaper in mud, but they were happy, entertained, and safe. A rarity in this house.

"It's so hot, I thought they might enjoy it. Don't worry, I'll clean them up." He picked up Artemisa to head to the outdoor water pump, but Tía blocked his path.

"You don't have time, the last bus is leaving soon." She reached into her apron pocket and handed him some peso coins, just enough for the bus fare. "We can't afford to keep you anymore. Give your grandmother our regrets."

Regrets didn't even begin to explain it. Santiago let the toddler slide down his body, leaving a trail of mud on his own bare chest and pant legs. His hand absently rubbed the burn marks still visible on his arm as he remembered the pain of the cigarettes from his last stay with his grandmother.

"But what about the babies? Who'll take care of them?" Santiago spoke without thinking. A shadow darkened Tía's eyes. He jerked his head back, and in that split second her hand missed contact with his cheek. Missing her target only raised Tía's anger.

"I'm their mother. You think I can't raise my own *hijos*? I got along *de lo más bien* before you got here."

This time Santiago kept his mouth shut. They obviously had a different understanding of "just fine." He remembered the last family wedding, during which the three kids had yelled continuously, been dragged out of the church kicking and screaming, and broken free to shove six greedy hands directly into the wedding cake, all while Tía had cried, swearing to Dios that she couldn't take it anymore. Yes, she got along *de lo más bien*.

It was *she*, biologically his grandmother but better known in his mind as *la malvada*, the evil one, who thought up the golden solution: send Santiago to his aunt and uncle's house to take care of the toddlers. Tía (though technically a second cousin, and not Santiago's aunt) had jumped at the idea of having a free babysitter, and *la malvada* marveled at getting rid of the grandson she despised.

Santiago hadn't complained. Honestly, this suited him

just fine. Sure, Tía blamed him for everything—the kids getting chicken pox, lice, diaper rash, runny noses, still not talking in full sentences, waking up in the middle of the night, not eating, eating too much—but at the end of the day, it didn't compare to the abuse of living with *la malvada*.

"Please, let me stay." Santiago held out his hand to return the bus fare, but his *tía* ignored it. "I'll take care of everything tonight; you relax. I'll bathe the kids, feed them—"

"There's nothing to eat, *idiota*," she reminded him.

"What if I get a job?"

"What job are you going to get when your uncle has no work?"

No answer came to Santiago. No one had work to offer; no one had spare money to pay someone for work.

Tía folded her arms across her chest and nodded to the *calle*. "*Lárgate.* Unless you want to walk the two hours all the way to your grandmother's house, you better go."

Santiago stared at the house that had been his home for the past seven months. In the room he shared with the three kids were clothes too small for him. His one possession, a small pocketknife, had been found in the road. The blade was dull, the scissors didn't open, and the toothpick and tweezers were missing, but it was his. Like all good pocketknives, it remained with him at all times.

He washed the mud off his hands and chest at the outdoor pump and pulled on the T-shirt he'd taken off before playing in the mud. Apolo stood up and lifted his arms, expecting to be carried, but Tía stepped in front of her children, blocking them from their babysitter. Artemisa scooped up a particularly gooey handful of mud and flung it at her mother's shoe. Tía didn't notice. Her attention remained on Santiago.

Santiago looked into the faces of each of the kids, faces that had worked their way into his heart. He raised his hand in good-bye. "Listen to your *mamá, chiquitines.*"

No longer able to look at them, he turned down the same road his *tío* had traversed moments before. In perfect synchronicity, the three kids broke into cries.

"Tago, Tago, *ven.*" Jesús called out the nickname he'd made up for his babysitter.

Apolo and Artemisa didn't say his name but kept up with the cries. Santiago slowed his pace, waiting for Tía to call him back, to say she would figure something out, just as long as he quieted the kids.

But his *tía* said nothing. Next door, the *viejita* shut her window.

CHAPTER 2

The coins Tía had given him burned in Santiago's hand. If he'd learned anything from his years of moving from one relative to the next, it was to spend money while he had it. Saving it would be the same as losing it. Or having it stolen.

The setting sun indicated there wasn't much time left. He hurried past the bar where his uncle would be filling his empty belly with beer and *chicharrones* until his money ran out. Even then, Tío would stay longer, in hopes that Tía would have calmed down and that the kids would be asleep when he returned.

Except the kids wouldn't be asleep. Not without Santiago there to tell them a story and rub their backs. Tía would very soon regret her hastiness in getting rid of him.

At the grocery store, he bypassed the line of people handing over their backpacks and large bags while they shopped, and headed to the bakery section. Since it was the end of the day, items there had been reduced to half off. The remaining bread rolls were smaller than his fist; he grabbed two from the plastic display case. In the meat department, he convinced the butcher to sell him a few scraps of raw meat; even one slice of cured meat would have been beyond his budget. Adding his meal up in his head, he figured he had just enough for a small bottle of Coca-Cola.

He handed over the few coins that had been meant to take him back to *la malvada*'s house forty minutes away by bus, received no change, and sat on a park bench to enjoy his meal.

Even with the stale rolls and the chewy, uncooked meat (his iron gut could handle anything), it wasn't the worst meal he'd eaten. He smiled. Life felt good and full of possibilities. Not that he knew what possibilities were out there, but returning to *la malvada*'s wasn't one of them. He'd decided that the last time he left her house.

The best part: No one would come looking for him. *La malvada* didn't have a phone so wouldn't know to expect him. It could be months before his *tía* and she saw each other again, and several more before mentioning him in each other's presence. When they figured out he'd gone missing, if he was lucky, they'd assume he was dead. If he was really lucky, he wouldn't be.

The night air sent a chill over his bare head. He tugged a short strand from behind his ear, wondering when it'd get long enough to curl again. A week ago Tío had pinned him down while Tía shaved his head for giving the kids lice. Truth was they'd gotten lice on their own.

He would need a place to stay the night, ideally not a park bench or under a bush, where a stray could pee on him.

He racked his brain for options until he had an idea. He'd registered the existence of the abandoned shack the first week here while walking the toddlers, complete with harnesses and leashes. Set back from the street, run down, no door, and half the roof missing, it seemed to serve no purpose other than to divert attention. Now the memory popped up as he searched through his mental shelter file.

His feet crunched on glass as he entered the shack. Lights from the street outside showed mounds of trash. The smell of urine indicated other humans had used this place as a sanctuary. But the wrappers were old, and the smell wasn't fresh.

Through a hole in the roof, a raindrop fell on his bare head. Only parts of the roof were missing, but the areas that would remain dry were also the ones littered with the most trash. Using his feet as a broom, he pushed the garbage to the exposed parts of the shack. He cleared a sleeping spot until only dirt remained under his feet. Settling down with his back against the wall, he hugged his knees to ward off the chill as he watched the light rain fall on the trash. A steady drop pinged against a glass bottle like a chime. As it always happened when it rained, and many times when it didn't, a memory came.

After a particularly hot and dry summer, when he was four years old, the sky had darkened into a sudden downpour. Everyone scrambled to get under portals or into shops. Mami instead had gripped Santiago's hand tight and turned her face up as if blessing the rain.

"Can you feel each drop land on your body?" Mami had said, her eyes still closed. "Washing away everything bad and leaving a fresh start."

"It's like taking a shower, but better," Santiago said as he opened his mouth to catch the rain. "Can we do this every day?"

"*Claro, hijo.* Any time it rains, we'll come out and celebrate it together."

Mami removed their shoes, and they pranced through the deserted town. Mud oozing through their toes, rain running down the back of their necks, they chased streams and sang silly songs. Though only four, Santiago could honestly say he had never had more fun than he had that day.

He also didn't remember dancing in the rain again. At

least not with Mami. And later it became forbidden. Only lunatics and vagabonds danced in the rain.

No, he wouldn't think about that. He focused instead on the ping of the raindrops landing on the glass bottle. But just as he knew it would, the next memory played automatically.

This time *la malvada* stood over him, cigarette drooping from her lip, as he swept the clumps of mud his *abuelo* had trudged in.

"Your feet are covered in filth like a pig's. Your *madre* was a pig too," his grandmother said. *La malvada* had a way of glaring at him as though he were some disrespectful kid, even though a growth spurt meant that he technically could look down on her. "Always running around barefoot. Everyone said she wasn't right in the head. Like we were to blame for ending up with such a nutcase. I tried to beat the crazy out of her, but once an egg's gone bad there's nothing to do but throw it away."

"Mami was not crazy," Santiago said. "She knew how to be happy and not end up like you."

La malvada's face twisted into an angry scowl as she flicked cigarette ash into his eye. "Life is about struggle; you're not meant to be happy. She was crazy and look where that got her. Burdening me with her impudent and *malcriado* son. You're going to turn out just like her. A waste of space and air."

Santiago rubbed his eye, the memory of the ash stinging as much as the event. The rain eased up, and the pings
against the bottle became less frequent. With arms folded
under his head to act as a pillow, he looked through the
patches of roof up at the sky. The remaining clouds combined with the light pollution made stargazing impossible,
but he knew they were there. Some shining bright, some
far and faint, some that had died out, but their memory still
glowed. Just knowing the stars were there, in some form
or another, made it possible for him to take a deep breath
and close his eyes.

CHAPTER 3

If there's one thing Santiago knew, it was there's no telling what will happen in the future. One second his *mamá* had been crossing the street, holding his five-year-old hand, and the next second a car had run a red light and hit her. In that split second of impact, she'd let go of him, saving his life even though she couldn't save her own.

Santiago didn't trust the future, didn't plan for it. Not when the future did what it wanted to, regardless of any efforts. Tomorrow or a week from now didn't matter. Instead Santiago lived in the present, and in the present his stomach growled.

Except he didn't want to leave his spot in the shed just yet. The morning sun glared down on him through the patches of missing roof. For a while he enjoyed the warmth on his body after the cool night, only getting up when his stomach threatened to audition for the tuba section of an orchestra.

In the center of town, near the plaza and a church, a food truck emanated scents of meat and spices, beans and roasted chile. A woman sat at a plastic table in the shade, her plate piled high with more food than Santiago ever remembered having. Inside the truck, a man leaned on his elbows to look out the service window.

For the past few days, Santiago had scrounged for food behind grocery stores and in trash cans, but now he had a better idea.

"Con permiso." Santiago excused himself to the vendor. "Is there any work I can do—wash dishes, take out the trash—in exchange for a meal?"

The man straightened up, shaking his head. "Business is too slow today; I've done everything. She's the only customer I've had." He gestured to the plump woman at the table.

Santiago nodded his thanks as he turned away. He could try other food vendors, but if this truck, the one with the best smells coming from it, didn't have much business, others wouldn't either. Most people here didn't have spare money to buy lunch.

"*Oye, chico*. C'mere and share this plate." The woman at the table beckoned him with her plastic fork.

Santiago hesitated long enough for her to roll her eyes at him.

"Look," she continued, scooting her plate in his direction across the table. "There's too much food here. Either sit down and help eat it, or wait to pick the remains from the trash." She scooped a huge forkful into her mouth and, while still chewing, turned to the vendor. "Now this is GOOD food."

Still not sure what she might do to him or what she would expect in return, Santiago gave in to his stomach pains and pulled up a chair beside her. She looked young, maybe nineteen or twenty. Her eyes, almost black yet bright, looked straight into his, hiding nothing. His *tía* never looked him in the eye, and *la malvada* hit him when he tried to look into hers. This lady, though, smiled and encouraged eye contact. She handed him one of the two tortillas as a scoop to help himself from the plate.

Pork and pinto beans, rice with lime and chile, tomatoes and zucchini with cilantro and olive oil. Tía had been a mediocre cook, and *la malvada* never gave him any food other people might eat; as he took a bite, he couldn't remember a meal that tasted so good.

"Right? I told you, good stuff, huh?" The woman took another forkful and shifted to address the vendor. "Can we get another Coke here?"

But Santiago stopped, the sky-high-piled tortilla rest-ing in his hand. Two eyes, dark and bright with extra-long eyelashes, appeared from under the table. Santiago gulped. He could blame the table and bright sun, his empty stomach, or anything else, but that didn't change that he had done exactly what he hated his relatives for doing—thought only of himself.

"I can't eat your food," he said, setting down the tortilla platter after only one bite. "There're two of you."

The woman waved her hand as if he'd said the stupidest thing in the world. "There's enough on this plate for all of us. Alegría, God help her skinny genes, won't eat any more."

The little girl, about four or five, straightened up and continued to stare at him through her long eyelashes while she gnawed a pork bone. Mouth and hands covered in meat juice, she offered the remaining bone to Santiago.

A lump rose in his throat as he insisted the girl finish the bone herself. Jesús, Apolo, and Artemisa never shared with anyone. If anything, they stole food from one another's plates and had learned to eat as fast as they could or be left with nothing.

"Please, eat," the woman insisted.

The vendor came over with the Coke and exchanged it for the coin the woman had left on the table. Still eating with one hand, the woman used the other to push the bottle across to Santiago.

"Gracias." The word caught in Santiago's throat. Thanking someone because he wanted to, because he felt truly thankful, that had not happened in a long time.

The woman shrugged off his word like nothing. "So, do you have a name?"

He finished swallowing before answering. "Santiago."

"Only Santiago? *¿Sin apellidos?*" she teased.

"Santiago García Reyes." He added his two last names. The one from his father, whom he'd never met, and his mother's. Everyone he knew had two last names, but sometimes people would skip mentioning one of them. If he ever skipped one, it'd be García, his father's, but never Reyes. He'd never skip Mami's.

"Hey, we're cousins! I'm María Dolores Piedra Reyes." Her eyes widened more as she kissed her daughter's head. "And this is Alegría García Piedra. We're definitely related."

She meant it as a joke, as people often did when they met someone with the same last name. Santiago stared at her to make sure they weren't really *primos*. Surrounding her face were full cheeks, so ready to smile. Her hair fell loose, midnight black from her scalp to her ears and then bleached blond until her shoulders. And of course her eyes, her happy, kind eyes. On her and her daughter. No one in his family had happy eyes. Not anymore at least.

"Are you from around here?" he asked, just to be sure.

"No, from Culiacán, near the coast. Can't you tell from

my voice?" Her accent wasn't one he'd heard before. She kept on talking without pause. "We're just passing through. Going to *el otro lado*, where my sister lives. She and her husband own a restaurant and asked if I could help them out."

"Sounds nice." He tried to hide the bitterness in his voice. That they had a place to go, that people wanted her and her daughter there. From the table he picked up a piece of zucchini that had fallen from his tortilla. He squashed it between two fingers then ate it. He couldn't waste food now when later his stomach would once again audition for the orchestra.

María Dolores continued, not worrying about speaking with her mouth full. "If you think this food's good, you should try my sister's cooking. I swear, she talks to her ingredients, and they return the favor by turning into meals that sing back. I don't have that talent. Instead, I excel at taste testing."

Santiago forced a smile at her joke and shoved the last of the piled tortilla into his mouth. The little girl, Alegría, once again offered him her bone, which still had a few bits of meat clinging to it, and once again he shook his head.

"You eat it, *chiquitina*." He smiled and nodded to her. "I'm getting full," he lied, but his thoughts turned in a new direction.

El otro lado. He could get a job there. According to rumors, even the lowest-paid jobs earned more per hour than the daily wage here in México; food was so plentiful, grocery stores threw items away when they got old. And best of all, it was far away from here.

He wiped his mouth with his hand and ran his tongue over his teeth to make sure no food stuck to them. Shoulders back and sitting up straight in the plastic chair to make a good impression, Santiago looked directly into María Dolores's eyes.

"I want to go with you two. To *el otro lado*."

CHAPTER 4

For the first time in the fifteen minutes Santiago had
known her, María Dolores sat mute.

"I want to go with you," Santiago repeated. "I'm strong
and fast. I can be useful."

"I'm sure you could, but I don't know you." She shook
her head, sad and apologetic, but sincere just the same.
"You don't know me."

"I know you're the nicest person I've met in a long
time."

"Doesn't sound like you know many nice people."

He looked at her without blinking. "No, I don't."

"Obviously, seeing no one feeds you. Here, finish the
rest of this." She pushed her plate forward. Santiago looked
from the plate to María Dolores, not sure what action

would let him pass the test. A piece of tortilla remained. He mopped up all the juices before pushing the few beans, rice grains, and a tomato onto it and handing it to the little girl. She dropped her finished rib on the plate and took a bite of the loaded tortilla remains before returning it to Santiago.

He finished the leftovers in one bite and threw the Styrofoam plate in the trash. He returned the empty glass Coke bottles to the food vendor and asked the man for a couple of wet paper towels before returning to the table.

"Do you want to wipe her face and hands?" He gestured to the little girl covered in pork juice.

María Dolores nodded. "Good thinking."

He used the other paper towel to wipe the table clean of dirt and food stains that hadn't come from them. His arm stretched across the surface to rub a stubborn spot clean.

"What's that?" María Dolores pointed to his side, right above his hip, where his shirt had ridden up.

"It's nothing." He tugged the hem of his shirt down. "Are you done with the wipe?"

María Dolores dabbed the corners of her own mouth before handing the paper towel back to Santiago. He walked the trash to the can, careful not to let his shirt ride up again.

"Why do you want to go to *el otro lado*? Do you have family there?" she asked.

No, but I don't have any here, either, he wanted to say. Instead, he grabbed for the first story that came to his head.

"*Sí*, my uncle. He needs my help running his shop. He's a good man, hard working, but he doesn't have any kids and he's getting old, so—"

"Really? Your uncle?" Her happy eyes narrowed, and she shook her head slightly. "Let me tell you something, boy. I'll put up with a lot of things, but being lied to, to my face, is not one of them."

Even with her narrowed eyes, she maintained contact with his. He didn't break it. The more the idea whirled in his mind to accompany her to *el otro lado*, the more he wanted to find a way to make her agree to it. Or he'd have to go on his own.

"You're right. I don't know anyone over there. But the people I know here are not ones I'll miss." His hand fell again near his hip, then dropped quickly when María Dolores noticed. He stuffed his hands in his pockets. "I don't know what I'll do once I get there, but I guess I'll be able to take care of myself better over there than here."

The woman continued to stare at him. Her eyes saddened as if he reminded her of someone. "I believe you, and I'm sorry that's the case. How old are you?"

"*Cator*—" He started to lie out of habit and say "fourteen" but then corrected himself. "I mean twelve. But I'm tall, so people think I'm older."

María Dolores brushed a lock of black hair from her daughter's face. "I was taking care of myself by thirteen, but everyone thought I was sixteen. I know what it's like."

He said nothing. Silence hung between them until she broke it.

"Are you a criminal?" She stared at him with her intense eyes, waiting to catch him lying again.

"No."

"Are the police or anyone looking for you?"

"I haven't done anything illegal, and no one will notice or even care that I'm gone."

She made a noncommittal sound in the back of her throat. He could see her caving, fighting the rational part of her brain that said it'd be crazy to travel with a strange boy to a strange country.

"Did I tell you I'm strong?" Once again he grasped for any quality that might convince her. "I can carry extra water and food, whatever you need, and I'm used to surviving on little. I won't eat much."

"More like you've never been given enough. Here." She dug into her purse, pulled out a small chocolate bar, and handed it to him. He broke it in three and let the little girl pick her piece first. She picked the biggest, as most kids would, and he grabbed the smallest before María Dolores could.

He sat on the plastic chair, straight and attentive as he

savored the chocolate, letting its sweet richness melt in his mouth. It had been years since his last taste of chocolate. Probably someone's birthday piñata, though not his. His birthday was never celebrated.

María Dolores finished her chocolate and then turned to her daughter. "What do you think? Should Santiago travel with us?"

By way of responding, the girl slid off her chair and walked to Santiago's, stopping with her right sneaker posed forward. "Can you tie my shoe, Santi?"

"Sure, with bunny ears?" He made two loops with the laces and recited the poem Mami had taught him about the bunny hopping along but then needing to hide in his hole to escape the coyote.

> *El conejo corre*
> *En su hueco se esconde*
> *Así el coyote*
> *No se lo come*

Once her shoe was retied, Alegría climbed onto her *mamá*'s lap and stared at Santiago with her wide eyes. "I like Santi, Mami. Is he my new brother?"

Darkness clouded María Dolores's eyes before she turned away. Two deep breaths later, she lifted her gaze with a forced smile.

"We'll see," she said, kissing her daughter on the cheek.

"So, Santiago." María Dolores pushed herself up from the table. She reached down between her feet and pulled out a plastic bag, its handles threatening to break from the weight of its contents. "We need some things from the market before we get on the bus. Do you know a good place?"

"Definitely!"

He had no idea whether she meant to include him in the "we" getting on the bus. She hadn't said no or sent him on his way, either. Good enough for now.

Santiago led them past the church and through a narrow alley where the skeletal dogs gave them hungry looks. They arrived at a market square a few minutes away that bustled with vendors shouting prices and holding out items for sale. Walking three abreast became impossible in the crowded and narrow passageways.

"Look, why don't you get us some groceries?" María Dolores eased them into a vacant corner after they'd been bumped and jostled a few times. "Big jugs of water, and food that won't spoil quickly. Bread for sure. Maybe some nuts if they're not too expensive. Some more Carlos V chocolate for me. Alegría likes the Haribo bears, so if they have a small packet. And something for yourself. We'll meet you there."

She pointed to the vendors selling cheap clothing, shoes, and handbags, and handed him two fifty-peso notes from her pocket. His fingers rubbed the paper, certain they were real, but still shocked. It wasn't really a lot money, but he'd never been entrusted to hold so much in his hand. If he wanted, he could run straight to the bus station and go far away with that kind of money. Far enough that no one would ever find him, at least.

But María Dolores trusted him. Or the money was another test. Either way, he wasn't going to let her down.

First stop, nuts. Being heavy, and sold by the gram, they got expensive quickly. Three stands side by side all sold nuts and dried fruit.

"How much for the shelled peanuts?" he asked each person, and all three answered the same price.

"But if you buy half a kilo, I'll give you ten grams extra." The man in the middle nodded to his scale.

"Or if you get them from me, I'll throw in twenty grams of raisins as well." The lady scooped her raisins to show him how they glistened in the sun.

The remaining vendor shook his head no.

"*Bueno*, the half a kilo of peanuts and twenty grams of raisins," Santiago agreed.

At the grocery store he calculated that four bottles each holding one and a half liters of water would be easier to carry than one giant bottle for almost the same price. He also got sandwich bread, brown, because he heard that was healthier than white, and found some cans of Spam and sardines on sale. He'd never tasted sardines, but the price was too cheap to pass up. The goodies for María Dolores and Alegría was inexpensive, so he treated himself to three pieces of his favorite *caramelos*.

He returned to the market square, arms aching from everything he carried. He found the mother and daughter trying on sneakers and set the goods near their feet. From his pocket he dug out the remaining coins: sixty centavos. No, that wasn't right. He rechecked his pocket and found the extra ten centavos in a corner. He wanted to make sure María Dolores knew he hadn't shortchanged her.

"You got all of that with *cien* pesos?" She looked up from where she pinched Alegría's shoe, making sure it fit.

"Yes. There's half a kilo of peanuts, which cost—"

"I don't need the tally. I'm just impressed." She pointed to a stand straining with every kind of footwear imaginable. "Now, take off your shoes."

"Mine?" Santiago took a step back, suddenly feeling vulnerable and scared. She couldn't take his shoes. He'd had them for almost a year; they'd belonged to a cousin before him. Not that he liked his shoes, or his cousin, but they were his and had been with him for a while. Besides, he didn't want her to see all the holes in his socks. Or gasp from the smell.

She ignored his question and held up a pair of brand-new white sneakers with orange interiors. "Do you like these?"

Of course he liked them. He'd never had new shoes. But this was too much. He didn't deserve this. And from his experience, gifts never came free.

"I don't need new shoes."

"Really? Your soles are coming off like they've grown mouths."

He looked at the shoes he put on every morning without ever noticing them. Sure enough, both shoes displayed his dirty socks like sickly tongues poking through. Maybe new shoes would be a good idea.

He sat on the bench and removed his mouth-shoes, trying to hide the state of his socks by keeping his feet tucked under the bench. But in a second, María Dolores pulled a fresh pair of socks off the stand and handed them to him. He disposed of the old, smelly socks without argument, pulled on the new ones, and slid his feet into the white and orange sneakers. His toes wiggled comfortably. The insole cushion molded to his feet.

"Do they pinch or anything?"

He wiggled his feet some more. "They're perfect."

"Good." María Dolores handed the vendor the old shoes to throw away or mend and resell at his pleasure. Santiago rocked his feet back and forth, overwhelmed by the comfort.

Along with the sneakers, María Dolores also bought (three!) new backpacks. When the vendor gave her the total cost, Santiago almost fainted. He opened his mouth to haggle down the price, but María Dolores spoke first.

"You forgot to charge me for his socks."

The man waved his hand to say that the socks were on him, except María Dolores insisted on paying him the full amount. What a strange woman. Santiago had never met anyone who didn't try to bargain. She didn't seem particularly wealthy—none of her clothes screamed brand names, and she didn't have that rich-person haircut. But she certainly didn't seem worried about money either. Very strange.

Maybe that's why they got along. His mother had been strange too.

CHAPTER 5

María Dolores insisted on buying him a new hat, T-shirt, and pair of jeans as well as the shoes. "You can't go around with your ankles exposed like that," she said in reference to his too-small jeans, and even he had to admit his original T-shirt was filthy; between the mud party he'd attended with his cousins and sleeping in the abandoned shack for several nights, its original color had long since disappeared.

"How can you afford to be so generous?" The words escaped his mouth before he could stop them. Now he'd done it. If he'd learned anything being passed from one ungrateful relative to another, it was to never mention money. He prepared to give up the shoes, the clothes, and the trip to *el otro lado*, when she laughed.

"I'm not rich." She gestured up and down at her faded jeans and T-shirt. "A few days ago, I made the choice to leave my old life behind and sell something I no longer wanted in order to get to El Norte one way or the other. I'm just getting what we need and hope I keep making the right choices to keep us safe."

Finally convinced they had everything, María Dolores let Santiago lead them to the bus terminal. The bus route she settled on took five hours longer than the direct one but ended up saving her thirty pesos. But then she bought them two huge sandwiches, and a roll for Alegría, all bursting with different meats and oozing with mustard.

"The thing is," she said, biting into her sandwich while they waited on hard plastic chairs for their bus to Capaz, "even though I don't have much, I like to support hardworking people trying to make a living. I know what it's like to survive on little."

"I try not to take from people who have less either," Santiago admitted, pleased that she talked to him like an equal, like an adult. "Where is Capaz anyway? Is that in *el otro lado*?"

"Nearly. It's where we'll cross. I've never been there, but my sister warned me it's like any border town: filled with crime and corruption."

"Sounds like my family," Santiago joked. Except it wasn't exactly funny.

María Dolores raised an eyebrow. "Trust me, my family is pretty screwed up too."

Once on the bus, Santiago watched the familiar town pass by. With each tire rotation, he felt lighter and happier than he remembered feeling in a long time. Buses usually meant returning to *la malvada*'s house. This time, on this bus, he was traveling far, far away. If that wasn't reason to smile, he didn't know what was.

"Santi, can you read this for me?" Alegría pulled out a coloring book from her new brown-and-pink backpack. A few sentences at the bottom of each page told the story of the characters, some of whom still waited to be colored.

He leafed through the pages. With the disappearing light, even the images were hard to see. From what he could tell, it wasn't a very interesting story.

"Can I tell you a secret?" he whispered in Alegría's ear. She widened her eyes while nodding excitedly. "I'm not very good at reading."

More accurately, he couldn't read at all. According to *la malvada*, Santiago would never amount to anything, so what was the point in spending money to educate him? For the most part he got along fine not being able to read—he knew what the food packages looked like and was great at directions without reading the street names. But at times like this, when there was a book to read and share, he wished he could.

"I can read my name," Alegría said. "And Mami's. I'll teach you."

"I'd love that." He smiled as he reached for a strand of hair that had come loose from her pigtails and tucked it behind her ear. "So, why don't we make up the story? It's about two bears, right?"

"Yeah! And they're scared of a bee."

"Exactly. Because the bee thinks the bears stole his honey when really they didn't."

They added to their story, introducing characters and events that weren't shown in the pictures, until the last page, where the bears and bee celebrated with a honey party.

"Again, again!" Alegría shrieked so loudly her *mamá* opened an eye long enough to see they were fine and shifted back to sleep.

"The same story?" Santiago whispered.

"*Sí, por favor,*" Alegría whispered back.

"Okay . . ." He pretended to sigh, as if Alegría would soon regret hearing the story again. She didn't. She had him tell the story four more times, adding new elements with each telling.

When *madre e hija* were both sound asleep, Santiago leaned back on the rear bench and relaxed but didn't close his eyes. The lights of each passing vehicle reminded him how lucky he was.

CHAPTER 6

They arrived in Capaz around three o'clock in the morning. Santiago held the sleeping Alegría with her arms draped around his shoulders and her head nestled into his neck. Even as he shifted her weight to follow María Dolores, who carried two of the three loaded backpacks out of the last bus, the little girl didn't stir. For a second he missed his three cousins. Even when they would shriek and cause mayhem all day long, they would always cuddle against him at night.

Then he remembered the screams and continuous accusations from his *tía*. She never hugged him. No adult did anymore.

The bulbs in many of the streetlamps had burned out, while others had been smashed, making the trek through the unfamiliar town unnerving. From what he could see, the town was nothing more than run-down shacks closed up for the night. Heavy iron grates or sheets of metal blocked the storefronts. Santiago started scouting for a safe place for them to stay until sunup, some alleyway or even a dumpster if it would keep the *ladrones* away. Two gunshots went off close by. Santiago huddled closer to María Dolores, half wanting to protect her, and half to be protected by her.

María Dolores looked at her phone for directions. She seemed to have a plan, even though Santiago didn't know what it was. They turned down a street to a tavern with a flickering green light that alternated between half-lit words. If it was anything like the tavern his uncle frequented, the place probably offered beer and beds.

The inside smelled of spilled alcohol, vomit, and unwashed humans. The bartender, bald except for some tufts of gray hair above his ears, looked up from his conversation with the only patron and jerked his chin upward to ask what they wanted.

"A room," María Dolores said. Santiago noticed the lone man on the bar stool eyeing them. Or more specifically, eyeing María Dolores. Hopefully this would be a place where rooms came with locks.

"How many beds?" the bartender asked.

"Two."

The bartender grabbed keys from under the bar and told his comrade he'd be back in a minute. As they walked away, Santiago still felt the other man's eyes on their backs.

The stairs creaked. Any second they'd fall through and land right back in the middle of the bar. Santiago shifted Alegría to keep her from slipping.

On the landing the bartender pointed out the bathroom and then the shower room. "Showers are extra, and you have to borrow the key from the bar. This is my place, so if you need anything else, the name's José."

Don José opened the door to a bedroom with two beds squeezed together in the shape of an L and no room for anything else beyond the space needed to enter. They received the key, and María Dolores handed him a folded banknote. Already what she'd paid for Santiago racked up to more than he remembered any family member spending on him.

María Dolores dumped the bags on one of the beds and eased Alegría from Santiago's arms to carry the sleeping child to the bathroom.

"Dead-bolt the door behind me and don't let anyone in," she whispered. "A place like this, bedbugs will be the least of our worries."

Santiago took off his shoes and plopped onto the free bed. It creaked when he shifted, his bottom sank into a hole in the middle of the mattress, and it smelled of old cigarettes. But it had a pillow. He couldn't remember the last time he'd slept with a pillow, even a flat one like this one. He stayed awake long enough to see the two return from the bathroom and hear the click of the door lock behind them.

CHAPTER 7

Voices from the midmorning crowd stopped talking the second Santiago, María Dolores, and Alegría emerged in the bar. A few of the men raised their eyebrows or winked. Santiago reached into the pocket of his new jeans to grip his dull pocketknife. He'd seen eyes like these before: on dogs ready to attack a stray chicken.

"Didn't your *mamis* teach you it's rude to stare? *Sin vergüenzas*," María Dolores called out, but Santiago noticed her grip on Alegría's hand tighten. In a no-nonsense strut, she went to an empty table and set down their bags, which they hadn't felt safe leaving in the room. Once María Dolores sat, Alegría slipped into her lap and buried her face in her *mamá's* chest.

"She's right—shame on you all." Don José emerged

from the stairs after them. "So either you behave or get the hell out of my cantina."

Everyone returned to their conversations, but Santiago could feel rather than see the late breakfast patrons still sneaking glances at them.

The old man shuffled to the bar and brought *café con leche* and a plate with three doughnuts to their table.

"I don't get involved," he muttered under his breath to them, "but I wouldn't trust most of these men with anything. Especially my life." Then he cleared the dishes from the neighboring table and wiped down the surface as the chef brought food out from the kitchen.

Alegría uncurled enough from her fetal position to enjoy a doughnut but didn't leave her *mamá*'s lap. The hairs on the back of Santiago's neck continued to send off warnings.

Two guys at the table to their left started talking in hushed whispers—whispers that were really too loud if they truly wanted no one to hear.

"They found six bodies in the desert the other day, fried to a crisp. It was that Domínguez. He tells these innocent people he can get them across at a good price and then abandons them in the middle of nowhere. Poor souls," the first guy said with an accent only found in pretentious telenovelas.

"People are really stupid sometimes." The second man spoke in a whiny voice.

Pretentious crowded closer to his friend, ready to divulge a huge secret. "We've got two spots left in the van tonight, but I think a pair from Puebla will take them."

"Is that the new van with air-conditioning?"

"Yeah, it's a sweet ride with Arizona plates," Pretentious agreed. "Crosses the border without a glitch, and everyone's in Tucson by the morning."

"What do you charge again?" Whiny asked.

Pretentious shrugged and waved his hand aside. "Oh, you know me. I just want to help these poor people reach their destination. I'm sure we can strike a deal that's, uh, comfortable for everyone."

Santiago slammed his coffee mug on the table. They didn't have to say it for him to understand they meant to take advantage of María Dolores. María Dolores narrowed her eyes; a quarter of the doughnut turned in her hand, like she wanted to chuck it at Pretentious's head. To Santiago's disappointment, she didn't.

Two different men got up from a far table and walked to the bar to settle their bill. As they passed, one of them casually dropped a piece of paper on their table. María Dolores snatched it up, scanned it, and hastily crumpled it in her hand.

Santiago leaned in and spoke in a whisper that even Alegría, still on her mother's lap, wouldn't be able to hear. "What did it say?"

"It's a marriage proposal," she whispered back.

"*¿Qué?*" Santiago blurted. Half the men turned to look at them again.

María Dolores sent him a silencing glare before whispering the rest. "He claims to be a U.S. citizen and would like to marry me. For a fee."

"*¡Qué locos desgraciados!*" This time he remembered to keep quiet.

"Agreed. I'm done here."

She paid for their breakfast, and they gathered their things to take back upstairs. Once in their room, the door locked, they kept their voices low. From the next room they could hear everything their neighbor said on the phone.

"I don't know what to do." With a sigh of defeat, María Dolores crumpled onto the bed. "My sister said once we got here it'd be easy to find a coyote to take us across the border, but she crossed with her husband. I hate it, but I'm scared. This is going to be harder than I thought."

"I don't like it here, Mami." Alegría sucked the left-over doughnut sugar from her fingers. "These men aren't nice."

"I know, *mamita*." She kissed her daughter's head before turning back to Santiago. "How can we find someone trustworthy?"

Santiago leaned against the closed door.

"Okay, how about this?" he said. The idea scared him, but the more he thought it through, the more realistic it would be to pull off. "I'll help out in the kitchen, clear tables, *o lo que sea*. As long as I mind my own business, grown-ups don't notice me. I'll keep my ears open and find a coyote we can trust."

"*El viejo* won't pay you to work," María Dolores pointed out.

"So? I'll tell him I'm bored and you want me out of the room for a while." Fear merged with excitement. He could do this.

María Dolores ran her fingers through her daughter's pigtails. "I don't know."

"It'll work." Santiago bobbed his head. "Those men were obnoxious. But others might come in later who aren't. I'll check them out and report back."

She sighed and agreed to the plan. "I've never had a brother, but if I did, I'd wish he were like you."

He reached for María Dolores's and Alegría's hands, giving them both a gentle squeeze, then letting go quickly, not sure if he'd overstepped some invisible boundary. "You two are pretty cool too."

He gathered himself to leave. At the door, his hand paused in midair above the handle. He turned, slowly. *Madre e hija* stared back at him.

"Will you still be here when I come back?" he asked.

"Of course!"

"¿Me lo prometes?" he whispered, addressing her for the first time as a friend, instead of a stranger.

María Dolores reached into her pocket and pulled out a black lava stone smoothed into a flattened heart. She placed it into Santiago's hand. "This stone has been passed down for generations in my family and was given to me by my *abuela* when she died. It's the most valuable thing I have, and I'd be heartbroken if I lost it. Hold on to it for me and give it back when you return."

She closed his fingers around the stone. It warmed his palm, like the lava still retained some life. The hearts of her ancestors. He didn't believed her story, but it was a nice stone. He could keep it safe for a few hours.

CHAPTER 8

Only a few heads turned when Santiago stepped down from the last creaky stair, and no one gave him more than a fleeting look.

Without asking, he grabbed a damp towel from the side of the bar and headed to the nearest empty table. He stacked the dishes into a neat pile, wiped down the surface, took the pile through the swinging kitchen doors, and set it in the sink. A plastic tub caught Santiago's attention. He could carry more dishes, making fewer trips back and forth. And spend more time eavesdropping. Someone once told him it was easier to beg for forgiveness than ask for permission.

"Mi hermana," he told the owner, testing out the strange word and enjoying how natural it felt rolling off his tongue. "Wants privacy and—"

"Do you hear me complaining?" Don José carried plates of enchiladas, tacos, posole, and rellenos to a large party crammed into one table. "Wipe that chair down too. I see beer dripping down it."

Conversations flew from all directions. He tuned out the ones about family members and life outside of Capaz and focused on those about crossing. As he moved his cleaning rag and gray bin from one table to the next, no one paid him the slightest attention.

A man to Santiago's right slapped a newspaper onto the table. "What the *pollos* don't understand is that there's nothing out there. No food, no water, no shelter."

His companion grunted in agreement. "Exactly why we don't need a wall out here. The sun takes care of everyone that doesn't know where he's going."

"*Oye, flaco,*" called a different man from another table. "I thought we lost you to the desert, *hombre.*"

"You almost did, you jerk." The two embraced like brothers. "*Los azules* picked me up and threw me in jail, thanks to you."

Santiago moved his bin to a table where a boy not much older than himself was drunk and weeping like a baby. "The bodies. Every time I close my eyes I see them. They were only out there for a half a day and hadn't even crossed the border."

"That's why they need someone like you who knows

the way, knows how to survive in the desert." His friend pushed another drink in front of him.

The crier took a swig. "But I don't know the way, and I don't want to die. I can't do this!"

"Sure you can. Come with me a couple more times and you'll know the route in no time. But it's always good to show the *pollos* the skeletons so they know they can't do it on their own."

Santiago had heard enough. Heaving the bin onto his hip, he headed to the kitchen. Anyone who talked so callously about dead bodies and used them to get business was not a coyote they would hire.

"Unload and come back out." Don José pointed to a table where four men sat with a clutter of empty dishes. These men, most likely brothers, shared similar features with sunken dark eyes and square jaws. Their haircuts indicated money, and the way they sat with their shoulders back showed their place in the world. A gold watch shone on each brother's right wrist.

Like the others, they didn't stop their conversation as Santiago approached and began collecting dirty dishes. Like he wasn't even human.

"We have to do something about Domínguez. He's out of line," said the bearded brother.

The oldest brother, and the one with the most jewelry, waved the concern away. "I don't think he's taken that much business from us. Especially after his incident."

"That's beside the point," Beard snarled. "He's ruining the whole chain of command we've established."

"Others see him and start thinking they can earn more by going rogue as well," the youngest brother piped in.

"Looks like Domínguez needs to be reminded of his place." The final brother, with a broken nose, mimed a gun being shot.

A gold watch flashed as the oldest brother slapped the other's hand. "No, you leave Domínguez out of this. Like him or not, he's family."

"Your wife's family," reminded the youngest.

"My family is our family. Don't you forget that." The oldest man turned and waved a finger for Don José to bring them a round of drinks.

The younger three men said nothing, but even with his head hung low, Santiago could feel looks being exchanged that their older brother didn't notice.

The table cleared and wiped down, Santiago moved to the next one just as Don José came with the beer. The conversation quickly changed to a baby's baptism.

Without finishing their drinks, the four men suddenly rose from their chairs and glided into the kitchen, the one with all the jewelry coming within a hair of knocking into Santiago as he glanced over his shoulder.

Officers entered the tavern in pressed navy uniforms and shiny black boots. Two of them carried rifles in their hands, and the rest (Santiago counted seven) all had handguns in their holsters. The other patrons, coyotes and immigrants, pulled coins and crumpled banknotes from their pockets to leave at the tables and inconspicuously disappeared from the bar, some through the front, but others through the kitchen's back door.

Santiago rested the tub against his hip and slid beside the owner to whisper, "Who are these guys?"

The old man didn't even look up from where he counted the coins left on the bar. "*La migra*. Border agents."

Santiago swallowed. "Ours?"

The agents pulled up chairs, and the ones with rifles rested them on their laps. The weaponry froze Santiago in place.

"Theirs. But don't worry, they don't have any official jurisdiction here." Don José slid the coins into his pocket.

Santiago watched *la migra* agents. Their faces, a mixture of brown and sunburned, seemed relaxed and unperturbed, but arrogant as well, knowing people feared them even outside their country. A greater need to be invisible overcame Santiago. Nothing good ever came from the presence of the police, regardless of what division or country they worked for. In his experience, once a cop, always a *perro*.

La migra greeted Don José in booming but completely incomprehensible voices. On a good day, Santiago only knew a few words in English: "hi," "bye," "thank you," and "Coca-Cola." Other days, some accents didn't even allow him to understand those words.

Santiago went into the kitchen, staggering from the weight of the bin.

"Wash those pots for me." The chef motioned to the pile he'd placed in the sink. "Every time people start using my kitchen as an escape route, I know who's arrived, and they all eat like pigs."

Not a minute later, Don José entered the kitchen with enough orders to feed twenty people. Santiago quickened his pace, scrubbing the pots and pans with steel wool and giving them a quick rinse before passing them back to the chef.

The owner watched him for a couple of seconds as he ate a few spoonfuls from a bowl of menudo. "I don't think our dishes have ever been cleaner."

Santiago shrugged as he placed a stack of plates to soak while scrubbing the last pot. He didn't know how to answer that; people didn't usually notice what he did or talk to him at all.

The owner set down the bowl and started flash-frying some tortillas for enchiladas. "There's plenty of menudo if you're hungry. Those lightweights out there won't touch it. Take a couple of bowls upstairs to your sister and niece. Anything you guys want to eat."

Was that a subtle way to get him to leave? But the dishes weren't done, and both of the men were busy cooking. "I still have work to do."

"*Un chile de todos los moles.*" He praised Santiago. "It's sure appreciated."

The bar got even busier once *la migra* left and the buses arrived. The people looking to cross, mostly men, but some women, teens, and children as well, stood out from the local smugglers. Some were curious and quiet, taking everything in. Others complained that they had paid too much money to stay in such a dump. Regardless of their demeanor, all of them showed signs of nervousness.

Now, with potential customers, the coyotes used every method of persuasion to get hired—fear, bribery, and machismo.

"You'll get lost and die without me. There isn't a town for over one hundred fifty kilometers once you cross the border."

"It hasn't rained in months, and it's hot enough to fry an egg on your bald head, but I'll carry an extra bottle of water just for you."

"Only the strongest, toughest people survive the desert.

I don't know if you've got what it takes to make it."

A man with a dark mustache sitting on a bar stool motioned Santiago away from the predators. At first Santiago pretended not to notice. During the whole day, none of the customers had paid attention to him other than to hand him an empty glass. But when the man waved again, Santiago shuffled over with the heavy bin of dirty dishes still in his hands.

"You're new," the man said, eyeing him up and down.

Santiago shrugged.

"'Bout time José got some extra help here," the man continued.

Santiago remained silent. He had wiped down the bar and cleared all the dirty dishes from it. As far as Santiago was concerned, there wasn't anything the man could want from him.

Not that the man cared. He jerked his chin toward the kitchen. "Do you know if *el cocinero* made any menudo today?"

"*Ey.*" Santiago found his voice.

"Well, see if you can find enough to fill up a bowl for me." He flicked a peso coin over the bar to Santiago.

Santiago pocketed the coin without thinking.

The pot of tripe stew sat on the far end of the stove, where it stayed warm without taking up a burner.

"There's a man who wants the menudo, and Don José

has gone upstairs. All right if I give it to him?" Santiago asked the chef.

In way of response, the chef quickly warmed up two tortillas in a skillet, turning them every few seconds with his bare fingers, and placed them on the plate next to the soup bowl.

Not a drop spilled as Santiago set the stew on the bar for the mustached man.

"I'll take a Coke, too."

Going behind the bar felt imposing, but the refrigerator holding the drinks hummed in plain sight. Santiago wouldn't have to snoop to retrieve a cola.

"Thanks, kid." The man placed a crumpled fifty-peso note on the bar.

What was he supposed to do with that?

"Don José will be down in a minute with the bill," Santiago said. He went to pick up a stray plate and almost got knocked over by a cowboy bursting through the flimsy screen door.

The cowboy stood there for a few minutes, scoping out the joint. Dressed in what looked like his best clothes—shiny boots, creased black jeans, blinding-white cowboy shirt, and tan cowboy hat—he looked ready for a wedding, or funeral. Santiago gestured at a few empty spots, but the cowboy continued searching for whomever he'd come to meet.

"I'm looking for Domínguez," the cowboy finally called out. "Where can I find him?"

The mustached man swiveled slowly on his stool until his elbows rested on the bar behind him. The fifty pesos were no longer on the surface. "Depends on who you ask. Why're you looking for him?"

The cowboy walked to the mustached man and dropped onto the bar stool next to him. He lowered his voice, but not so low that Santiago couldn't hear. "He got my brother and nephew across a few months ago. But since I've gotten here, everyone's been saying that Domínguez has the highest death rate of all the coyotes combined."

The mustached man reached around for his Coke and nodded in understanding. "People believe what they want. Sometimes truth is subjective."

The cowboy wrinkled his brow under the hat brim. "I don't know what that means."

"It means just because you think one way and someone else thinks another, doesn't mean both aren't right." He raised his Coke at the cowboy, toasting him before taking a swig.

Several seconds passed before the cowboy shook his head. "You speak in riddles. Do you know where I can find Domínguez or not?"

The mustached man shrugged. "If I tell you, are you going to trust him to take you across?"

"Maybe? I don't know." The cowboy sighed.

"So, think about it. If you want to hire him, I know where to find him. If you decide he's not the guide for you, then we've both lost nothing." The mustached man raised his empty Coke bottle at Santiago to indicate he wanted another.

The cowboy stood up to leave. But then he started a dance of returning to the bar stool before changing his mind, heading to the door, and then sitting back down a couple of times before he finally left the tavern.

"Poor man wouldn't know where to take a dump if he came across two toilets side by side," the mustached man said with a smirk as Santiago set the second Coke in front of him.

Santiago returned behind the bar and used his rag to clean up a spill he hadn't noticed from the other side. "You're Domínguez, aren't you?"

The mustached man twisted the cap off the bottle and took another chug before answering. "It's possible. Common name, after all."

The indecisive dance the cowboy had done proved to be not so crazy after all. Santiago could see the risk. After all, rumors often got started from truth. But from the conversation Santiago had overheard from the gold-watch guys, it sounded like they hated Domínguez because he didn't play by their rules.

Not playing by the rules didn't make someone bad. Especially if the rules were unjust to begin with.

This man, Santiago could tell, had experience, obvious by the comfort he had in his own skin and his take-charge attitude. In Santiago's mind that implied he knew how to do his job: He could get them across. He also didn't prey on the *pollos* like the others did and was the first coyote who hadn't made Santiago's skin crawl. He hated to admit it, but Domínguez had also been the only customer to see him as a person.

But was all that enough to put his life, and the lives of María Dolores and Alegría, in this man's hands?

"Could you take us to *el otro lado*?" Santiago asked, still not convinced but willing to hear more.

"Who's 'us'?"

"Me and my sisters." He realized his mistake as soon as he said it. If they wanted the lie to be believable, then he'd have to say that Alegría was his niece instead, like Don José had assumed. But even though he'd never had a sister, nor a niece, he liked the sound of having two sisters. It felt better too.

"How old?"

"Nineteen and five." Or close enough.

Domínguez shook his head. "Nah, I don't like taking

the little ones. Too dangerous. They can't run fast."

"So you think we're better off going with someone else." Santiago said it in disappointment, but Domínguez interpreted it as a bartering tactic.

"Son of a gun, no." Domínguez shook his head. "You're a sharp kid, you know that? Twisting things around to get your way. A lot like me."

Domínguez drank from his Coke again before turning back to Santiago. "*Mira*, here's the deal. Crossing the border with a five-year-old is hard; I won't lie to you. You could all die trying to save her. You might die anyway, even if you didn't have her."

Crossing without Alegría would mean going without María Dolores, and he wouldn't be here in the first place had he been alone.

"It's either the three of us or none of us." This time Santiago knew what he was implying. He might not like or trust any of the other coyotes who'd frequented the tavern so far, but that didn't mean they weren't options.

Domínguez reached into his pocket for a pack of cigarettes and a lighter. After the first drag, he turned back to Santiago. "Guess you and your sisters are better off with me than one of these punks hanging around here who thinks north is straight up into the clouds."

Santiago smiled slowly as he raised his eyes from the now clean workstation. "Does that mean you'll take us?"

Domínguez grumbled. "I'll consider it. But I don't work for free. It's ninety-five hundred pesos. Per person."

Santiago's stomach contracted as if someone had punched him in the gut. That much? Each? He'd been so desperate to leave his past life, he'd forgotten about a crossing fee. María Dolores must have assumed he had the money to pay for himself. For the first time in his life, he agreed with *la malvada*—he was a no-good, begging, *lentejo*. Expecting something for nothing.

Santiago hid these thoughts as he nodded, indicating he never expected it to be cheap. "My older sister handles the money. She's upstairs. Can I send her down?"

The cowboy returned, boot heels clomping with determination as he stomped back toward them.

Domínguez sighed and rolled his eyes at Santiago as he muttered, "I don't like this, but yeah, go on and get her before I change my mind like this *idiota*."

CHAPTER 9

The chef urged Santiago to finish off the menudo to empty the pot. Enough remained to fill two bowls. Santiago mopped up the sides of the giant pot with a flour tortilla and ate that himself while the chef warmed up more tortillas to place on the plates under the bowls. Santiago walked slowly up the stairs, careful not to spill a drop. He paused outside their bedroom door—he'd left without the key, and knocking with two hot bowls of stew in hand seemed impossible.

"María Dolores, it's me. Open up. I brought lunch."

No answer.

No footsteps heading to the door.

The bathroom door stood ajar, and no sound of running water came from the shower room.

He balanced on one foot and used the other to knock while calling out again. A trail of broth spilled from one of the rims and burned his thumb.

Still no one answered.

"María Dolores? Alegría?" The words choked him, or maybe it was the silence that followed.

They'd left him, abandoning him even after that stupid story about the lava rock. If he had a free hand, he'd get rid of the stone right now. It always happened—people got tired of having him around. He should be used to it. But it'd been a long time since someone he liked had left him. Two someones he had started caring about. It just proved that the only one he could trust was himself.

"Santi, over here!"

He whirled around so quickly, half of the menudo spilled from the bowls he still carried. Through the dark hallway came Alegría running toward him with María Dolores smiling behind her. The little girl hugged his legs.

"José moved us to a nicer room. Didn't he tell you?" María Dolores said.

Santiago shook his head, not daring to speak.

"This one's got a bigger window and enough room for a pitcher of water and a mirror. We're talking a high-end suite here." With her hands outstretched, María Dolores reached for the bowls of stew before stopping short. "What's wrong? Are you crying?"

Again he shook his head and kept his face down so she couldn't see.

"*Ay, cariño.*" She handed Alegría one bowl and held the other while she reached to put her free arm around his shoulders. He shifted away. "It's okay; we're here."

She motioned for him to follow them through the hallway and into the new, bright room. The blinding light gave him the chance to shut his eyes for a few seconds. He took two deep breaths before rubbing his eyes open.

"Eat. The food's getting cold." He leaned out the open window. The sun blazed down on the top of his head and into the alley, where two cats pawed through the trash.

"Santiago." María Dolores spoke softly as she walked up to the window. "Can you talk to us?"

He pushed away from the view and curled up on the far bed, his back against the corner, arms over his head. "I found you a coyote, but he charges a fortune. If you can afford it, you two go. I'll stay here. I think Don José might let me work for room and board."

He heard María Dolores start to say something then stop. Instead, the clink of spoons against the bowls filled the room. After a few minutes, a gentle tug on his shirt made him look up. Alegría took that opportunity to crawl into his lap.

"Santi, have you met Princesa?"

"No?" The response came out as a question. Whatever

he thought Alegría would say, it hadn't been that.

"She's right here." The girl pointed to the empty space next to them on the bed. "She's my best friend, but she only speaks Unicorn."

Santiago straightened up further and held out his hand to let the invisible unicorn sniff it. "She's very beautiful."

Alegría nestled closer against Santiago's chest. His fingers absently ran through her pigtails, ready to untangle any knot.

"Yes," Alegría agreed. "But she's a little scared."

"Why is Princesa scared?" he asked.

"She thinks you'll forget about her."

So Alegría understood what needed to happen, what he needed to do. He wouldn't forget about her—either of them—but better that Alegría forgot about him.

"Did you know it's okay to be scared?" The words had been Mami's, but he'd said them a few times to comfort his cousins. "Being scared means you have feelings, that you care. And because you care, that lets you be brave. So I know Princesa might be scared, but she's also very brave, right?"

"*Sí.*"

An arm wrapped around Santiago's shoulders. His body tensed as María Dolores rested her head against his. He caught a whiff of fruity shampoo from the two girls' heads.

"I think you need to remember your own words," María Dolores whispered in his ear. "It's okay to be scared, and to care. That's part of your bravery too."

Words rose to argue with her—that wasn't what he meant at all. And besides, he just said it to comfort the five-year-old.

He felt an impulsive need to break away and flee, but he was stuck. He'd have to leave, eventually, but a few more minutes would be okay.

"Do you really want to stay and work in the tavern?" María Dolores again spoke quietly, her head still next to Santiago's.

"No." He lifted Alegría from his lap and slid off the bed, unable to have them there so close any longer. "But you need to take care of *ustedes dos.*"

"How much money does the coyote want?"

"Nine thousand five hundred pesos *por persona.*"

"So?"

"That's nineteen thousand pesos."

"Three times nine thousand five hundred is twenty-eight thousand five hundred."

"You can't spend that much money on me!"

"*Mira.*" She got off the bed and took his chin in her hand so he'd look at her. "You asked to come with us, and I agreed. That's part of the deal. I knew what that meant. But let me say, if you want to stay with us, you have got to stop thinking we're going to leave you at any moment."

He tried to look away, but her hand remained under his chin. He averted his eyes. "It's that—"

She shook her head. "I don't care. We look after each other. You found a coyote; I take care of the finances. It all works out."

"But you said you're not rich."

"I'm not," she agreed. "I got my first job at eight and was kicked out of the house at thirteen. I've had to work hard most of my life and put up with a lot of bad things to get here. But I also know money isn't everything. It buys neither happiness, *ni amor*. I can't take it with me when I die. I might as well use it while I have it. Otherwise, what's the point?"

He struggled to see the logic of that. All his life he'd heard what a burden he was, how expensive it was to keep him fed and clothed. But here María Dolores seemed almost indifferent to money. It didn't make sense.

"You don't have to understand what I'm saying." Her tone softened. "I just want you to know that I get to decide how I spend my money. If that means getting the three of us across the border, then I'm doing that, because I think it's worth it. You're worth it."

He saw no benefit in disagreeing. What he'd do was simple: He'd help them get to *el otro lado*. Once there, he'd go to some rich city and get a job that paid him thousands of pesos a day so he could pay her back. They say every-thing is possible in *el otro lado* if a person works for it.

"You have to come with us, Santi, have to." Alegría hugged his leg, sitting on his foot.

He nodded.

María Dolores smiled and gave him an affectionate shove on the shoulder. "So tell me, who's this coyote that's taking the three of us? Don't say it's that Domínguez."

CHAPTER 10

The sun blazed bright and hot when they piled into Domínguez's ancient, rusted station wagon the next day. The indecisive cowboy sat in front with Domínguez, still dressed in his fancy duds like he was ready for a date. Another man—Luis, from Central America by the sound of his accent—shared the back seat with Santiago, Alegría, and María Dolores. The little girl got her own seat because María Dolores said it wasn't safe for her to ride on her lap. A married couple, Tano and Vivian from the city of Chihuahua, occupied the rear-facing seat in the way back of the station wagon. Despite the intense sun, Domínguez promised the car operated on four-hundred AC—roll down four windows, drive a hundred kilometers an hour, and you had air-conditioning.

Before they left Capaz, Don José had pulled Santiago aside. "You've been a big help. If you think of it, send me a postcard from wherever you end up in *el otro lado*."

Santiago averted his eyes. "What if we don't make it?"

Don José waved that possibility away. "You guys'll be fine. You know I don't get involved, but Domínguez is one of the few good ones. I've watched him his whole life. He knows the desert, and better yet, knows how to survive in it. Listen to him, and he'll get you there safe."

Then he handed over three ice creams from the freezer behind the bar. Under one of the *paletas*, Don José included a folded slip of dull green paper. It showed an old-fashioned-looking white dude in the middle and numbers he recognized: $20. But it looked nothing like the colorful twenty-peso notes he was used to with a white background, blue and red ink, and a less old-fashioned Benito Juárez on the right.

"Are you sure?" he asked as Don José headed toward his customers. From what Santiago had heard, this note was worth a lot more than twenty Mexican pesos.

Don José narrowed his eyes and shot sideways looks across his tavern, reminding Santiago that anyone could be listening. "No one buys the *frambuesa*. Too exotic."

He had a point. Santiago had heard of "raspberry" but had never tried it in any capacity. He started to tuck the twenty dollars into his pocket but changed his mind. Too easy to steal, or lose. He let one of the ice cream bars drop to the floor. With the pretense of picking it up, he stuffed the money down his sock.

Now in the car, the raspberry *paletas* long gone (though Alegría still wore the evidence of red "lipstick"), Santiago could feel his foot sweat where it touched the paper money. The rest of him felt surprisingly comfortable despite the hot air blasting through the open windows.

"We're heading west, not north," said the cowboy up front when they turned from the main road onto a rutted dirt track.

Domínguez nodded. "*Tienes razón*. We are heading west."

"But we need to go north," the cowboy insisted. "It's called *El Norte* for a reason."

"And you don't think we're heading west for a reason?" Domínguez gestured to the barren dirt road in front of them.

"You're deliberately getting us lost before you abandon us, aren't you?" the cowboy accused. "Leaving us to die like you did those other guys."

Vivian, the woman seated with her husband Tano in the way back, called out, "Could you please tell us, Señor Domínguez, what really happened to those people who died?"

Domínguez lit a cigarette and took a drag before

responding. "Rumors say I abandoned them. Really, they were dying already. Fools brought beer to celebrate the crossing instead of water. Everyone knows alcohol dehydrates. Then we got caught in a dust storm for a full day. All that and the heat, I knew they wouldn't make it any further. I went to get them some help, telling them to stay in the shadow of a few boulders. I returned later to find them scattered and dead from exposure. Don't know anyone who could have done different, and many who wouldn't have bothered returning to look for them."

"You should have died along with them. Murderer!" the cowboy wailed.

Domínguez slammed on the brakes, almost sending the cowboy through the windshield. María Dolores braced herself against the back of the passenger seat while her left arm flew out to block Alegría and Santiago from sailing through the middle. Luis, the man next to Santiago, knocked his head against Domínguez's seat. Only the couple in the back sitting in reverse wasn't jostled.

Domínguez's cigarette fell to the ground as he burst out of the station wagon and walked around the car to open the passenger door. "Get out."

The cowboy shifted nervously, glancing around the dry landscape. No brush or boulder offered more than a few centimeters of shade. No sign of civilization existed in any direction. He curled his body over the seat-belt buckle.

"No, you can't do that. You can't leave me. I paid you."

Domínguez pulled a wad of money from his pocket and held it under the cowboy's nose. "If you think I'm a murderer, take it and get out."

"I'm sorry, please, no. I didn't mean it. Please, don't leave me here," the cowboy sobbed.

"Then shut up, and stop pretending you know how to do my job better than me. Next time I have to stop the car, I will kick you out." Domínguez punted a rock in demonstration.

"Excuse me, Señor Domínguez," Vivian called out again. "Since we've stopped already, is it okay if I pee really quick?"

Domínguez muttered a few bad words under his breath before jerking his head in consent. "You won't find much privacy, but take five minutes anyway. After that, I'm leaving."

The couple climbed out of the back along with Luis, and María Dolores rushed off with Alegría. Santiago exited the car only to get away from the cowboy, who remained with his seat belt still fastened.

Domínguez dusted off his dropped cigarette and walked a few meters away from the car. He kept shifting in a tight circle, attempting to relight his cigarette, but even with his back against the breeze, he struggled to get a light. Noticing his distress, Santiago walked over and cupped his hands around the flame. A couple of seconds later a puff of smoke came from the mustache covering Domínguez's mouth.

"I knew I liked you," the man said by way of thanks. He offered a cigarette to Santiago, who shook his head. Cigarettes reminded him too much of *la malvada*.

Instead he took in the barren landscape of northern Chihuahua. Dirt, sand, and stones dominated the terrain more than vegetation. Even the cacti and other spiny plants were sparse in this area. A couple of birds flew overhead that knew where to find enough nourishment to continue living in the desert.

"Maybe I should pee too," he said once Domínguez had gotten halfway through his rescued cigarette. "How far are we from the border?" He hoped the question would come across as conversational rather than demanding.

"About a kilometer or so." Domínguez puffed out some smoke. "But we'll drive right alongside it on this track for another hour. Around Capaz, there are too many eyes and ears. I know one guy who always walks his *pollos* right to the border patrol outpost on the other side, and *la migra* just drives them straight back to México. But the *desgraciado* has the people's money and a free ride back home, so what does he care? Makes it hard for the rest of us, just trying to make a living." Domínguez shook his head in disgust.

Santiago nodded sympathetically.

"So does that mean those mountains are in *el otro lado*?" He pointed north to a range in the far distance.

Domínguez took a deep drag as he nodded. "Yup. Those are in Nuevo México. Steep and dangerous to cross, but it's also the most direct way to Valle Cobre on the other side. Old mining town. Should be there in two or three days. Because it's hard to get to from this side, *la migra* usually doesn't bother with it. No buses run there, and cell phone reception is non-existent in that valley. But they have a working pay phone. Call someone to get you, and you're home free."

"Is that where we're going?" Santiago took in the mountains, studied their shape and ridges, how one part had a rock face that went straight up as if something had removed a slice. But he also imagined a town on the other side with chickens and goats scattered around the pay phone in front of a rickety shop that sold overpriced, out-of-date snacks.

"Not sure. Depends on the little one."

Santiago's defenses shot up. "She's tougher than she looks. And I'm not going to let anything happen to either of them."

"From what I've seen of you, I believe that." Domínguez threw his cigarette onto the ground and walked back to the car. "Pee break's up. You all got thirty seconds to get back in the car."

Small embers from the cigarette sizzled in the dry grass

around it. Santiago smothered them out with the toe of his new sneaker before joining the rest.

The cowboy still hadn't moved from his spot in the roasting car other than to fan himself with his hat. Domínguez took one look at him and shook his head.

"Switch places with the kid. I'd rather have him as my copilot."

The cowboy didn't budge.

Domínguez grabbed him by the shirt collar, leaving grime on his immaculate crossing outfit. "I will not say it again."

The cowboy hastened to unfasten his seat belt, but instead of going through the open car door, he crawled over the seats, afraid that once outside, he'd never be let back in. Santiago didn't doubt that the thought had crossed Domínguez's mind.

A pang of guilt went through Santiago as he fastened the seat belt in the front. Up here he had plenty of room on the bench seat and good air circulation. The back seat was now filled with three adults and a child; María Dolores didn't trust the cowboy and put herself between him and Alegría, meaning the little girl who couldn't touch the vehicle's floor had plenty of space while her *mamá* in the middle struggled for legroom.

Sorry, Santiago mouthed, but María Dolores shrugged it off.

Once the car got back in motion, Domínguez chatted to Santiago as if they were the only ones there. He pointed out the fuzzy mullein plant that could be used as wilderness toilet paper and warned about eating the flat cactus pads, *nopales*, which, while tasty, needed to be properly harvested to prevent the tiny prickly glochids, or "hairs," from embedding in the mouth and tongue.

"See those two fingers sticking out in the mountain range? Down between those two rocks there's a slot canyon with a nice cave. We'll ditch the car soon to cross the border, and we should get to the cave sometime tonight. That's where we'll sleep off the heat of the day tomorrow. It's harder to see, but night travel beats the heat."

In the sky, the sun still shone intensely. If Santiago had to guess, he'd say they had about two hours before sunset. And then a whole night before sunrise; the two fingers along the same mountain range Santiago had asked about earlier were much farther away than he'd thought.

"And then?" Santiago asked, wanting to add to his mental map.

"And then—What the—"

A cloud of dust loomed behind them, and from it charged a white SUV. Domínguez accelerated with a burst, jostling everyone in the old station wagon. From the back seat, Alegría began to cry in fear, and some of the grown-ups did too.

Low to the ground and on a rutted track, the old station wagon couldn't compete with the modern SUV built for off-road clearance, which soon began to overtake them.

A window rolled down, and the flash of a gold watch and silver gun barrel gleamed in the sunlight.

"Get down!" Domínguez yelled as he yanked the steering wheel hard.

BANG!

The car swerved off the track. Too fast, too sharp, the vehicle hit the dirt on Santiago's side while the other side rose in the air. He hugged his arms over his head as everyone screamed. The car continued hurtling through the air until it slammed to a stop and the glaring sun went out.

CHAPTER 11

Blood and sweat stung Santiago's eyes as he blinked. His hands searched in front of him and found shards of broken glass.

"María Dolores? Alegría?" His voice came out in a croak. Indistinguishable moans and cries responded instead of words.

He wiped his eyes and tried to figure out why the ground was so close to his pounding head. The seat belt had done its job, holding him fast and secure, but upside down.

It took some maneuvering to squeeze out through the open window and into the fresh air. Only the slightest speck on the horizon reminded him of the white SUV that had shot them off the road. Most of the station wagon's roof had collapsed as it lay belly up with its wheels spinning slowly. Smoke came from the hood, and some part of the motor still made noise. Any minute, the car could explode.

On his hands and knees, Santiago crawled over to the back-seat window. He could just make out the ball that was Alegría. Glass fragments still remained along the edges of the frame from the window that only rolled down halfway. He removed them quickly before lying flat on his belly to reach into the narrow opening.

"Alegría, it's me, Santi. I'll help you out." He kept his voice calm despite the adrenaline coursing through his veins. "I got you, *mamita*. I got you."

He couldn't tell if she even heard him over her cries. At least she was crying. Silence would have been worse. He eased her out, her fingers digging into his arms. He looked her over quickly, relieved to see nothing more than a few scratches and bruises, while she cried into his ear with her thin arms almost strangling him.

"*Mamita*, I have to help your *mamá* and the others," he said soothingly, stroking her hair, not knowing whether her heart or the pain in his head pounded louder than her cries.

But she refused to let go, wrapping her legs around his waist and locking her feet against his back. Like a possum, she held tight even as he peered into the overturned car.

"María Dolores, are you okay?" A tangle of legs

and arms made it unclear what belonged to whom, and whether they were still intact.

"I'm not sure," María Dolores mumbled. Some of the body parts shifted. Bleached hair stood out against the dark interior to finally reveal her face, also scratched and dirty. "Yes, I think so. But I won't fit through that window. The frame is too smashed up."

He tried the door; it wouldn't budge. With Alegría still clinging to him, Santiago rushed to the other side of the car. Luis crawled out from a slightly larger window opening while the mechanical noise from the engine continued to click.

"My arm!" the cowboy wailed from inside the car. "I think it's broken. I can't move. The seat belt won't come undone. It's so hot, I'm dying!"

"*Cállate ya*. No one who's really dying has that kind of lung capacity," María Dolores scolded.

"Here." Santiago crouched down to the warped window and pulled out his dull pocketknife.

The cowboy took it and tried to saw the seat belt. "I can't do this left-handed. It's useless," he whined.

"Oh, give it here." María Dolores grabbed the knife from his hands. "I swear, my five-year-old is more resourceful."

The belt took forever to snap free, and still the cowboy couldn't get out. His broken arm apparently gave his whole body the limpness of a banana peel. Between María Dolores pushing from inside, Luis pulling the good arm, and Santiago grasping a handful of the no-longer-white shirt, they finally hauled the yowling cowboy out of the car.

Bangs and muffled sounds came from the back of the station wagon, where the couple was trapped—the rear glass remained intact. With a few pulls and kicks, Luis opened the hatchback and set them free. But the collapsed roof prevented María Dolores from climbing over (though now under) the seat to escape.

"¡Santi, *fuego!*" Alegría cried in his ear. Santiago jerked around. Smoke engulfed the entire hood of the car, but no flames had formed. Yet.

María Dolores thrust her arms through the window. Her shoulders got through fine, but then she got stuck.

"Leave her," the cowboy said, cradling his arm. "We're all going to die anyway."

No, Santiago refused to let that be the case. Refused to give up and let her die halfway through a window.

"Please help me." He motioned to Luis.

The two of them slid their fingers between María Dolores's side and the window frame. With Luis's help, Santiago pulled back part of the warped frame with all the strength he had. He had to free her. Still wrapped around his body, Alegría pressed her weight against his chest. The gap widened a bit, then a bit more. Slowly, and carefully, María Dolores eased herself out.

She inhaled deeply before crawling over to kiss Alegría, kiss Santiago, and kiss them both several times more for good measure.

Until she stopped short. "Domínguez?"

They turned to look at the driver, and it became clear why they hadn't heard a sound from him.

CHAPTER 12

For several minutes no one said anything. Even the car's mechanical noise stopped as the smoke began to clear.

"What are we going to do now?" the cowboy demanded.

In response, Luis reached into the overturned car and pulled out his backpack. "I've come too far to stop now," he said in his southern accent. "Domínguez mentioned the slot canyon below those two rocky fingers. I'll see whoever there tonight."

He set off without waiting to see if anyone wanted to travel with him.

"Fool," the cowboy called out. "Crossing the desert on your own is suicide."

"Yeah, so what's your plan, *sabiondo*?" María Dolores demanded.

He held his immobile arm across his chest like some kind of salute. "I'm staying right here. If you're lost, you stay put so someone can find you."

María Dolores reached for Alegría, who held out her arms to be transferred from Santiago's. "Who do you think is coming for you? The guys in the SUV? Or the girl you're so dressed up for?"

The cowboy's face burned red.

"I think we should head back to the main road," Tano said. "At least that road *tiene movimiento*. Someone will help us from there."

"And then what? Go back to Capaz to find another idiot to get us nearly killed?" The cowboy continued raising a fuss. "I gave all my money to Domínguez. Actually, I should get it back."

Vivian raised her eyebrows in surprise. "You're going to steal from a dead man?"

"I paid him to do a job *que no cumplió*. I demand a refund. Besides, he doesn't need it anymore."

Santiago turned to María Dolores. As much as he didn't want to retrieve the money, he would if she asked him to. And she surely would. With three of them, she'd paid—and lost—the most. For her, after everything she'd done for him, he'd frisk a dead body. If she asked.

Which she didn't.

Instead, she taunted the cowboy. "Go ahead, get your money back."

But the cowboy didn't budge.

"That's what I thought," María Dolores said.

She jerked her head at Santiago. But away from the crash site, not toward it. Again, he marveled at her strange attitude about money. Had it been his cash they'd lost, would he take it back? He honestly didn't know.

They walked a short distance from the others and kept their voices low. She boosted Alegría back on her hip, keeping the five-year-old from sliding. "What do you think we should do?"

"The cowboy's right," Santiago said. His head gash no longer hurt, but another ache took over in his heart: responsibility for these two. "From the stories I heard at the cantina, crossing the desert alone, not knowing where we're going—we won't make it."

"We're not alone." María Dolores rested a hand on his shoulder. "We have each other."

Warmth spread through Santiago's body that had nothing to do with the blazing sun. But he shouldn't encourage desert travel on their own. It could go terribly wrong in so many ways. Those *migra* officers he'd seen with the rifles. He'd overheard one coyote in the tavern mention something about tear gas. Then there were the natural dangers: heat, fatigue, dehydration.

Still, the normal brightness in María Dolores's eyes had returned. "We have food and water for a couple of days. Plus a phone with a full battery."

"You won't get reception here." Santiago clung to reason.

"No, but I might on top of that mountain range. My sister is expecting a call once we cross; she won't be more than four hours away, driving. Maybe less."

"I don't know. Maybe we should go back," he said. But the idea of being in the crosshairs of those SUV thugs didn't appeal to him either. He had definitely seen a gold watch along with the gun; he remembered the three thugs in Capaz plotting against Domínguez, despite the fourth brother's rebukes. Santiago may have been invisible while clearing their table, but that didn't mean they wouldn't recognize him.

"You really want to return to Capaz?" María Dolores dropped her voice lower.

Going back to Capaz would be that much closer to going back to his old life. No, not an option. Even with the fear of the desert, forward was the only way to go. Especially with María Dolores's words beating like a mantra inside his head: *We have each other.*

"Domínguez did tell us where to go." Santiago worked

on convincing himself. "And I'm good at finding my way around."

María Dolores accepted that as a decision made. They walked back to the others. "We're checking out the border and trying to cross. Unlike our other friend, we will wait for you if you want to join us. There is safety in numbers."

Tano nodded. "You can come with us instead. My wife and I are going back to the main road, where we know someone will come along."

"Well, I can't go anywhere in my condition, and you can't abandon me to die." The cowboy gestured to his busted arm.

"We're not sacrificing ourselves to babysit you. You make your own choices," María Dolores said as she set Alegría on the ground and reached into the overturned car to retrieve their backpacks. The smoke from the hood had blown away completely.

Santiago went over to help, careful not to look into the car at the driver. Something red caught his eye near the damaged driver-side. Domínguez's lighter. Right there at his feet. Santiago pocketed it. Domínguez wouldn't mind. It had been there, in the dirt. Almost like he was meant to find it.

Once he straightened, Alegría tugged at his hand to be picked up again. Instead he crouched to her level and spit a few times into the hem of his shirt. Carefully he cleaned the blood from the few scratches on her face.

"There, now you don't look like you've been in a car wreck." He threw her up into the air and caught her as she giggled.

"*Mamita*," María Dolores asked Alegría as she held out the three bags, "are you going to walk?"

The little girl snuggled into Santiago's neck; her cheek muscles against his throat contracted into a smile.

"I don't mind carrying her. She's so light, I barely notice." He threw her up again before he reached for his bag and threaded his arms through the straps one at a time. Between Alegría in the front and the backpack in the rear, the weight balanced out nicely. It also helped that Alegría rested on his hips and didn't hang from his shoulders. From the bags, María Dolores extracted their new baseball hats—green for Santiago, grayish purple for Alegría, and rusty brown for her.

"Good luck." María Dolores waved at the others after settling her backpack on her back and Alegría's on her front. Santiago walked at her side, and the three of them headed toward the two fingers of the distant mountain range. To the north.

They had barely taken ten steps, when the cowboy called out, "Wait for me!"

Santiago stopped and turned. The cowboy ran to join the married couple as fast as his fancy boots and "broken" arm allowed him to go. Relief washed over Santiago.

Once they were clear of the crash site, but still with no visible signs of the border, Alegría squirmed down from Santiago's arms. She ran this way and that as she chased lizards and insects. From the corner of his eye, Santiago could have sworn he saw a glittery creature chase after her. Princesa. Maybe the invisible unicorn would look after them. He reached for María Dolores's hand and received a squeeze as each step they took brought the mountain range clearer and closer.

CHAPTER 13

El otro lado

No river or wall met them at the border. Instead, they only came across strands of a barbed-wire fence that had been cut. One strand rose, attacking Santiago's leg when he accidentally stepped on it, but it didn't even tear a hole in his new jeans. Was that it? Nothing more than broken wire to mark an invisible line in the sand and parched grass? Santiago thought he would feel something when he crossed, but he didn't. Everything remained the same. The same desert sun beat down on them. Nothing changed in the landscape. Even the mountain range seemed just as far away as before.

They kept the setting sun to the left and carried on.

A dirt road cut from east to west. Unlike the rutted

one Domínguez had driven on, this one was wide, level, and clear of debris.

"Stop." María Dolores flung her arms out to keep Santiago and Alegría from crossing the road. "It's a trap."

"How can you tell?" Santiago looked at the road carefully. There were no wires that might cause them to trip, and nothing indicated a trigger that would sound an alarm. In fact, he saw nothing on the road other than dirt and dust. Even rocks were scarce.

"Look." She pointed to the thin lines that went along the whole road. "It's perfectly grated. And soft. Anything that crosses it is immediately detectable. See over there? Some critter made those paw prints, and we can see exactly which direction it went. If we cross, *la migra* will know we were here."

Now that he looked closer, he saw other animal prints, but not a single one made by a human.

Maybe this was the real border. A test to see if they had what it took to cross seven meters undetected.

Behind them, the desert ground was so dry and compact, their shoes had barely indented the dirt. One step on the road, and their prints would light up like a beacon. Definitely trapped.

"We're not going to be able to get around it." Santiago couldn't see where the track ended to the east, and to the west the setting sun prevented good visibility. "The road probably connects two *migra* outposts. It's too wide to jump."

"So we're going to have to cross it. Exactly what they want us to do." María Dolores squirmed.

"What if we walk backward across the road?" Santiago demonstrated a few steps, which got Alegría hopping in reverse and trying to land where his feet had been, like backward hopscotch. She laughed at the complexity of the game, several times landing on the shrubby mounds of brittle grass instead of the spot where Santiago's foot had been. Santiago and María Dolores didn't laugh. When they crossed the road for real, it wouldn't be a game.

"We could try walking backward," María Dolores agreed. "And stepping in each other's prints isn't a bad idea either. People going to war would do that to hide their numbers."

"I can also wipe our path clear if you think that will help." Santiago picked up some twigs from a chamisa that on a windy day would become a tumbleweed.

María Dolores didn't say anything, and by that, she said everything. Santiago could read her mind—she didn't think it would work. *La migra* were probably trained trackers and not easily fooled by silly tricks. But she also didn't have any better ideas.

Santiago moved his bag to the front and this time carried Alegría on his back. María Dolores started crossing the groomed road, her backward footsteps sinking deep into the loose dirt. One careful step at a time, Santiago followed with the chamisa broom, trying to sweep away the evidence of their crossing. Didn't work. From a distance, a driver would see their jagged path across the track in a second.

Once across, María Dolores turned to face forward again and broke into a jog.

Santiago held Alegría's legs and jogged after.

"*¡Dale, caballito!*" Alegría squealed like she was riding a pony and wanted him to go faster.

The uneven ground of desert shrubs and small clumps of brittle grass challenged the run. A few times Santiago's ankles twisted, but not enough to cause real pain. Their scuttle gradually slowed until it became a walk and then a quick stop for water.

Once refreshed, they kept a fast pace. Every few minutes Santiago would pivot, turning to look in all directions for anything amiss. Lizards scurried by; insects buzzed and hummed. At one point he spotted a pair of vultures circling to the south.

Rest in peace, Domínguez.

The sun glowed bright against the ground, making it almost impossible to see to the west. Almost. Something moved in the glare, causing the hairs on the back of Santiago's neck to rise.

"Car." The word came out of his throat like a growl.

They scrambled for shelter. María Dolores crouched behind a gray chamisa bush while Santiago eased Alegría off his back and into the long shadow of a branchy cholla cactus. She lay flat on the ground, and he draped himself on top of her, his forearms supporting his weight. A few dropped cactus spines dug into his hands.

"I don't see it." María Dolores tried to peer around the bush.

"Trust me, it's there." He could almost feel the vibrations through the ground, his body on full alert to the danger.

The sun hid the dust, and the vehicle traveled slowly.

"It's coming," Alegría said, and was met with two quick *shhh*s.

The border patrol truck didn't travel by any road or path, or even in any obvious direction. North for a bit, then east, north again, briefly west, south, and then back to north.

Finally it stopped a hundred meters away. Santiago slowed his breathing, determined not to let his chest move. The sun had half disappeared, the shadows more then covered them, but who knew what kind of equipment *la migra* had to detect their prey.

A crackle came from the radio. Between his nonexistent English and the static, Santiago had no idea what they said, and he didn't dare shift his head toward María Dolores to see if she understood.

Two voices came from the truck as they discussed what to do. More static and robotic voices came from the radio. The truck returned on its jagged course, this time south. Then east until nothing, no dust, no vibrations, no alerts of danger.

They waited a few extra minutes before easing off the ground. Santiago pulled the cactus spines out of his and Alegría's hands. Only a faint glow from the sun remained. By the time they orientated themselves to continue north, that last sliver had disappeared.

"We've got to get to that cave," María Dolores said. "We're too exposed out here."

"I can still see, and the moon should be out soon."

Santiago led the way, careful to walk around the small, foot-level cacti and not trip over rocks. Even with the sun gone, the mountain range finally appeared to be getting closer. What he couldn't see anymore were the two rock fingers. But they had been to the left of the rock face that looked like it had been sliced in half, and that he could still see.

He kept up a steady pace with Alegría on his back and María Dolores behind. A couple of times she passed him a handful of peanuts and raisins and reminded him to drink some water.

Every once in a while, lights appeared on the horizon, but they vanished quickly and never headed in their direction. Beyond that, nothing disturbed the natural desert. No light pollution in the distance, just a billion more stars than Santiago had thought existed, a partial moon, and critters of the desert night. If he'd had the chance, he would have loved nothing more than to sit on a rock and enjoy the nature.

Santiago turned to María Dolores and grinned.

"*¿Qué?*" she asked sharply, her eyes darting around for danger.

He picked up her hand and gestured with the other at the panorama. "We've done it. We're here in *el otro lado*."

She let out a deep breath that she seemed to have been holding for days. Squeezing his hand, she returned his grin. "We made it."

A large mesquite stood in front of them at the foothills. Two reflective eyes close to the ground stared at them for a second before disappearing into the darkness. Santiago skirted the mesquite to find that it guarded the entrance to a narrow slot canyon. The rocky fingers from the ridge high above weren't visible from this angle, but his gut said this was the canyon Domínguez had mentioned.

"Hold on to us," he told María Dolores. Her hand joined Alegría's on his shoulder as he slipped into the rock crevice of the narrow canyon walls. The moon's light didn't reach the canyon floor, and only a strip of stars shone above. He walked blindly with his arms outstretched against the jagged rock walls and dragged his feet across the canyon floor to detect obstacles. His eyes adjusted a little to the darkness. Not enough to see his feet, but enough to notice a large shadow to his left.

From his pocket he withdrew Domínguez's lighter. The glow showed an indent in the canyon wall. A few more steps revealed an empty cave.

Tonight's home.

CHAPTER 14

Alegría barely shifted when Santiago eased her off his back onto the dirt. Only her head rolled to the side as she gave a little snore.

"Next time remind me how stupid it is to go hiking in new shoes," María Dolores said while beating her sneakers against the ground to soften the stiff backs. "How are your feet?"

He rocked back and forth in his new shoes as if he'd just put them on. "They're fine."

A couple of flicks from the lighter confirmed they were alone. Luis from the car hadn't found the cave.

"Should I light a fire?" Santiago asked after the lighter almost burned his fingers for the fourth time. A fire, he hoped, would also mask the smell of his offending feet when he removed his shoes. It worked when his gassy *tío* lit a match after leaving the bathroom.

"Do you know how?"

"Sure." Someone, Domínguez maybe—if this really was his designated cave—had stocked the cave with twigs and a couple of larger branches. "*La mal*— I mean, a relative's stove needed to be lit every day to cook. Some mornings I had to be up three or fours hours before sunup so the cooking could be done before it got too hot."

"Is she the one who hit you?"

He tugged his shirt even though the cave remained dark, and turned his back to her voice. He lifted his arm to search for a draft. There, a hole in the rocks and the slight oily residue of soot on the sandstone indicated a natural chimney. By feel, he reached for the small twigs he'd noticed during the last flick from the lighter. He then shaped them into a peak, adding tufts of dry grass and bark. "She did not always hit me. As I got older, she preferred throwing things—bricks, knives, boiling water. Or if I got too close, use me as an ashtray."

He broke a fat branch into thirds against his thigh and added the pieces to his pile of twigs and debris.

"But I didn't always have to live with her. Sometimes she could convince a different relative to let me stay with them, instead. I lived with an uncle who was great. Drunk all the time, but a happy drunk. Instead of getting angry,

Tío Bernardo just sang. Then one night he turned on the stove when he got back from the bar and set the house on fire. Neither of us got hurt, but we had to return to her house. He doesn't sing anymore."

Santiago lit the bits of dried grass at the bottom of his mound. They caught and began to burn the twigs and thin branches. The heat began to rise, and the flames grew stronger.

"When the last relative didn't want me anymore, I decided I wasn't going back." He fed the fire a few more sticks.

"What happened to your parents?" María Dolores placed a hand on his shoulder. He ignored her touch and watched the shadows from the flames dance against the cave wall.

"I never knew my dad. Relatives say he was a no-good *chulo malcriado*. Mami never mentioned him, and she died when I was five."

With the fire going strong and bright, he took inventory of the cave. Narrow in the front, it opened up to a larger space big enough for six or eight grownups to sleep side by side. In some places it was as tall as two men standing. Alegría continued to sleep, grunting occasionally, and María Dolores kept her eyes on Santiago. As if she really cared what he had to say.

"What do you remember of your mother?"

He leaned back on his heels, enjoying the comfort of the fire and the heat it brought despite their long hot day. He'd never talked to anyone about any of this. "Little things. She didn't care what people thought about her. Sometimes we'd walk through town singing off-key at the top of our lungs. Other times, we'd stop in the middle of the road to save a beetle. She was always in a good mood and liked to point things out. Birds, interesting clouds, the color of the dirt."

"She sounds like she lived freely. I wish I could have met her. What was her name?"

He smiled and let the name roll off his tongue. "Sofinda. I've always thought it's a pretty name."

"It is."

"Sofinda Reyes de la Luz," he said.

A half breath, half sigh escaped him as he sat on the ground and finally turned to look at María Dolores. "Why did you decide to leave?"

This time María Dolores turned away. "I was with a man who didn't treat me well. Alegría never liked him. I should have listened to her."

María Dolores lifted a pant leg to reveal scars on her shin.

"The first time I let myself think it was an accident. The second time I knew we had to leave. He went into a horrible rage and told the police I'd stolen from him. The engagement ring was mine to sell; he broke his promise to care for us when he hit me. That's how I've been able to afford everything. A friend got us out of town and we traveled east instead of north so he couldn't find us."

That explained the scenic route to Capaz. It hadn't been to save money, but to evade detection.

"María Eugenia, my sister, kept telling me to come live with her. She married a nice man, and they run a restaurant. She makes the best enchiladas *suizas*. I swear, I'd give anything for a plate right now." She handed Santiago a bit of chocolate, which he gladly accepted.

"I'd be happy with just arroz con pollo," Santiago said with a sigh. "No matter how bad you cook, that's one thing that's hard to mess up."

María Dolores let out what sounded like a laugh, but sad and bitter. "Trust me, it's possible. I have mastered the art of burning raw rice. And I'm talking completely raw, not the chunks of sticky burned rice at the bottom of the pot that I used to demand when I was younger."

"Pegado," Santiago said. At least that's what *la malvada* called it. As if giving it a name made it appetizing. He didn't realize other kids requested sticky burned rice.

"Yeah, love it, can't make it. My ex used to say I was useless because I couldn't cook."

"Was that Alegría's father?"

"No." María Dolores gave another of her part-laugh, part-snort sounds. "That was the ex I told you about. My *mamá* and I fought a lot about Alegría's *papá*, so I got kicked out of the house."

Santiago wanted to say he felt sorry for her—she'd gone through so much—but the words seemed empty. No one had ever shared things with him before, and he wasn't sure about the correct protocol. "Alegría is lucky to have you. You're the best mom for her."

"I'd like to think so." María Dolores smiled, pulling him close. This time he didn't flinch or resist. "Did I tell you she was the one who pointed you out when you walked over to the food truck? She liked you from the start. Recognized you as a good egg."

She gave him a teasing nudge. He slid a bit until his head rested against her shoulder. She hugged him closer and kissed him on the top of his head before whispering, "You'll take care of her, right? If something happens to me?"

He straightened up, breaking away from the embrace to look her in the eye. "You're dying?"

"Oh, no. But just in case, 'cause you never know. That's the problem of being a *madre soltera*. I want to know she'll be taken care of. That I'm not the only one she has."

He stood up to feed the fire another branch. A few insects fluttered around the flames, debating how close they could get before getting burned.

"I won't let anything happen to her, I promise," he said, returning to his spot, but not close enough for her to touch him again. "But I don't want anything to happen to you, either."

"So you'll stay and live with us?"

Stay? With these two and the older sister in *el otro lado*? In a real home? *"Claro que sí."*

"You won't leave?"

"Not unless you want me to."

"That will never happen."

CHAPTER 15

The sun shone hot and bright when Santiago woke up the next morning. His vision blurred as he looked up and down the narrow canyon walls, scoping out the landscape. Domínguez had mentioned it would be challenging but worth it to reach the old mining town of Valle Cobre on the other side of the mountain range. Except the SUV changed their plans before Domínguez had indicated how to get there.

Santiago followed the slot canyon to the end, staring at the ground for traces of footprints. He found nothing and soon he realized why. Not too far from the cave, the walls narrowed until he couldn't go any farther. The vertical rock walls reached for the sliver of blue sky without offering a single path or sufficient protruding rocks to climb.

Exiting the way they'd entered the night before, Santiago scouted the base of the mountain for footpaths over the range. Nothing stood out; nothing indicated the best way over. Large rocks dominated near the top, but he couldn't tell from the bottom how to get past the boulders. The range went on for a while in both directions; going around wasn't possible. On the plus side, not having any visible pathways meant *la migra* wouldn't know where to follow them.

All through the scouting, Santiago gathered branches and skeletons of dead cholla cacti to replenish the firewood in the cave. María Dolores met him at the cave entrance with two slices of bread with Spam and ketchup from a packet she had found in the bottom of her bag. After eating only peanuts, raisins, and chocolate last night, this felt like a gourmet meal.

"We don't have as much food as I thought. It might be a few days until we get to civilization. But we need to eat or we won't get anywhere," María Dolores said as she fixed a Spam sandwich for Alegría.

"How are we with water?" Even with all his scouting, he had seen no evidence of water anywhere. Just an arid, barren landscape as far as the eye could see, and a sun that would fry a lizard if it stood still long enough.

María Dolores showed him the remaining three bottles and sighed. "We went through more than a bottle yesterday. We need to make the rest last."

He told her what he'd seen outside the canyon. Or rather what he hadn't seen: trails.

"Princesa will help," Alegría said as she pranced around the cave with her imaginary friend. Santiago would have given anything to depend on a unicorn.

"Domínguez didn't mention offhand any other landmark?" María Dolores asked.

Santiago searched his brain for a few minutes. "Only the old mining village with a phone on the other side of the mountains, but it's hard to get to."

María Dolores made a sound in the back of her throat, part sigh, part growl. "I think that's our best bet. Keep heading north. Sooner or later, we'll have to come across something. A road or town."

He nodded, knowing they were both hoping for sooner rather than later.

"It's too hot right now, but I don't know if we can find our way over the mountain in the dark." He touched the back of his neck. Even now, in the cave, he could still feel the sun's heat against his skin.

"Let's wait a few hours and see how far we can get. We can stop once it gets too dark and start again first thing in the morning before the heat settles in." María Dolores stood up and took inventory of their things in the cave. "Help me pick up our trash."

She also made Santiago put on sunscreen.

"But I'm brown—I don't burn. And I'm wearing a hat," he protested.

"Doesn't matter. At least the back of your neck and tops of your ears. And your arms. It'll prevent heatstroke."

It sounded like an old wives' tale to him, but it wasn't worth resisting if it made María Dolores happy.

They started climbing the mountain in the late afternoon, zigzagging across, which was easier than going straight up. Alegría trotted from one direction to the next, chasing lizards and crouching to look at interesting flowers that flourished despite the desert heat.

The first hour or so proved the hardest. Santiago could feel the heat rising from the scorching ground through the soles of his new shoes. Had he still been wearing his old mouth shoes, he doubted his feet would have survived. Yet María Dolores insisted that they keep going. They passed the point of tired and uncomfortable and went on autopilot, keeping the same steady pace, often with Alegría holding Santiago's hand as Princesa guided the way.

The journey grew steadily rockier as they got higher; their steps caused small rocks to give way and create landslides. Twice Santiago slipped and landed on his knees. It happened many more times to María Dolores. He looked for a walking stick for her, something that would stabilize her footing. But no trees grew up here, and every stick he found snapped at the slightest pressure.

As the sun set, their way became blocked by boulders. Santiago lifted Alegría up and over the massive rocks, climbed over himself, and then offered a hand to María Dolores.

At the summit of the mountain, they finally paused. Half the night had passed, and the autumn breeze felt refreshing once Santiago removed his backpack. More mountains scattered the northern horizon, more empty land, more signs of desert, but no signs of water. No lights from a nearby town.

They settled among the north sides of boulders that felt cool to the touch, unlike the south sides, and blocked the wind. María Dolores emptied a backpack and placed it over Alegría like a blanket. A few hardy plants grew in the rock crevices, but none were sufficient to start a fire with. Back against a boulder, María Dolores placed a hand on her daughter and held her other arm out for Santiago. Too tired to resist, he curled up next to her.

The lightening sky woke Santiago up. His bones ached from the night's chill and sleeping on rocks, but still he scrambled back up to the top boulders. It took a few minutes, but there, finally, he noticed something. A faint line of a road running behind a hill.

Wherever it led, it gave them a more precise destination than just "north."

He memorized the shape of the hill the road went

behind—a completely flat mesa top with symmetrically sloping sides. He returned to their camp to find María Dolores awake and holding out her phone as she turned in a slow circle. "I've texted my sister, but I can't get a signal to send the message."

She handed him a piece of dry bread. He ate it slowly to trick his stomach into thinking he was eating more.

"I found a road," he said, licking his chapped lips. "I hope it leads us to Valle Cobre, where Domínguez said there's a phone and shelter until someone can pick us up."

Santiago reached into his bag for some water. Another bottle was completely empty, the third half-empty. Only a little more than one full bottle remained when yesterday they had almost three. He and Alegría had been so careful, taking the smallest sips. How could they have gone through so much without knowing it? He stashed the water back in the bag without drinking. María Dolores, still circling with her phone, noticed nothing.

"Let's walk before it gets too hot." He put on the backpack and lifted the sleeping Alegría into his arms. The wind tugged at her pigtails, ready to lift her up and carry her away. A sudden panic pulled in Santiago's heart at the thought of her being swept away like the townspeople from his favorite childhood story. He placed a protective hand on her back. Safe. He had to keep her safe.

María Dolores took two deep breaths and refilled

Alegría's backpack. At some point in their migration, Santiago had become the person in command, the person who knew where they were going. Or pretended he did.

They set off down the ridge and over the foothills. The chilly night gave way to another scorching day. They stopped before midday next to a low bush that provided the illusion of shelter but no actual shade.

Santiago slowly scanned the horizon. His vision blurred in the sunlight. It took several blinks to confirm that no trees grew out here; nothing but the hats and the clothes they wore protected them from the intense sun. Was it better to keep walking in this heat, or let the sun dehydrate them more as they did nothing? He couldn't decide, so they stayed put. Just for a little bit. The girls didn't complain either.

The crying yips of coyotes jerked Santiago awake. His throat burned with thirst, but he only allowed himself one swallow of water. They had to keep going. About an hour of sunlight remained, and they had to get to the road. All roads led somewhere.

"Wake up, time to go." His voice came out in a croak.

"I don't want to," Alegría whined.

"Can't we rest a little bit more?" María Dolores begged.

"No, we're not safe here," Santiago insisted, and they finally relented.

The second the sun disappeared, the air chilled, bringing goose bumps. In his arms, he could feel Alegría shivering. He rubbed a hand up and down her thin back and forced his stride to lengthen. Their destination had to be getting closer. Had to.

He led them blindly through the night. Several times he pinched himself to focus, only sometimes his brain reacted. *Water, shelter, freedom. Alegría, María Dolores.* They were what mattered. They were the ones he had to keep alive. *Keep going.*

The sun began to rise when they finally stumbled upon a faint trail. Turning his back to the sun, he followed the path into the hills. Maybe it was a mirage, a hallucination brought on by his extreme fatigue or cold, but something like a building loomed ahead.

"Veo una casa," María Dolores said, the first time anyone had spoken in hours.

It wasn't a house, at least not anymore, but a wall, made from mud-red adobe bricks. Santiago eased Alegría down before crashing onto the ground right next to her. Another rustle indicated María Dolores had done the same.

CHAPTER 16

Santiago's lips stuck to his teeth when he woke up.
His skin, exposed to the beating sun above him, stung from
sunburn. Just moving his head shot pain through the rest
of his body.

He took a swig of water before realizing that it was
the last of it. The fuzz in his brain slowed his reaction. Bad,
very bad. Up above him, three or four birds circled. Vultures. Something had died nearby.

Or was dying.

Santiago turned to María Dolores and Alegría lying
next to him. It took a few minutes to reassure himself that
both chests were rising and falling. The wall they'd used
for shelter early this morning no longer protected them
from the sun. Using the backpacks, he tried to build a wall

to cast a shadow over the sleeping figures. It barely made a difference, but it was something while he looked for water.

He forced himself to stand, dragging his feet behind him. *Keep moving, keep looking. Find something.* Except only the walls of a few structures made from thick adobe bricks surrounded the area; most of their wooden roofs had long since rotted away. No trash, no footprints, no sign that anyone had been there for years, maybe decades. This wasn't Valle Cobre, but some kind of settlement, abandoned and forgotten.

He closed his eyes, willing himself to hear the faintest sound of vehicles or, better yet, a stream. Nothing.

"Santiago, where are you?" María Dolores's voice crackled like she had a cold.

"Ya vengo." He shuffled his way back. Both of the girls were awake, and they grabbed him in a hug when he appeared around the wall.

"I thought you'd left us," María Dolores whispered in his ear. "I thought you'd . . ." That he'd left her with all the remaining supplies, in hope they'd somehow make it without him. He knew, because he'd thought of doing just that.

Instead he delivered the bad news. Nothing among these abandoned structures would help them survive.

"I don't know where we are," he said, kicking up dust on the faint trail that led to these ruins. "Don't know where the road to Valle Cobre is."

"I'm thirsty," Alegría said.

María Dolores reached out for her daughter, looking like she was about to cry for not being able to help her. "Our water is gone, *mamita*. My phone's dead. Don't know if my sister got the text or not."

The focus in Santiago's mind sharpened just a bit. He had to take care of them. Had to.

"We can't do anything now," Santiago said. Once again the sun blazed hot and bright. A few more hours and they'd be nothing more than human jerky for the vultures. "When it gets dark, we'll walk down the path we came up yesterday."

María Dolores swallowed and agreed. "Where do you think the path goes?"

"To a bigger road." He fought to keep the uncertainty out of his voice. "It'll lead us to a town. A real town with people and resources." That made enough sense to be true. "But first, let's rest in the shade."

He led them to an abandoned three-sided building that still had a partial metal roof. The dehydrated dung indicated it had once been a stable. Santiago moved a rotted piece of wood out of the way only to drop it again. He yelped as he and María Dolores jumped. Only Alegría crouched over to peer at the scurrying hairy legs of a tarantula the size of her hand.

"*¡Qué linda!*"

Once Santiago's heartbeat returned to normal (and Alegría moved the wood again, disappointed not to find any additional arachnid cousins), they opened the small can of sardines to share. They told Alegría to close her eyes and eat two when she refused, and then they shared the oil the fish had been swimming in. The grease soothed their raw throats and gave them the illusion of having drunk something.

At first Alegría didn't want to rest. She and Santiago colored in her book and told stories about the characters. Santiago could feel his mind begin to drift.

"Have you ever played Quiet Mouse, Still Mouse?" He remembered the game he used with his toddler cousins to help them nap.

Alegría shook her head, widening her eyes.

"So, we both lie down, and we have to be as quiet and still as possible." He lay on his side, using the crook of his elbow as a pillow. His other arm went around Alegría as she cuddled against his chest. "If one of us wiggles or talks, the other person wins. If we both stay quiet and still, then we both win. But I have to warn you, I'm very good at this game."

"Princesa and me are both really good too," Alegría said.

"I'm glad, because I could use a challenge. But you know, if Princesa starts moving and loses, we still have to see who gets second place."

Alegría nodded. "When are we starting?"

"Right now."

The little girl shifted to a more comfortable position and then didn't move again. Within a few minutes she was softly snoring.

The moon shone bright and almost full by the time they walked down the dirt track that would, they hoped, lead to a main road.

Only a few peanuts and raisins that had fallen to the bottom of a backpack and the three *caramelos* Santiago had bought for himself remained of their food supplies.

But no water.

They had packed food for a couple of days and were at their fourth or fifth day? Santiago had lost track. They finished off the last of their supplies—three peanuts and two raisins each. Except Santiago gave his raisins to Alegría. They completed their final meal by each savoring a square *caramelo*, which only reminded them of their thirst.

In a ditch next to the path something caught the light of the moon. Santiago held on to Alegría as he reached through the debris and pulled up a white plastic water jug.

"Is that water?" María Dolores gasped.

Santiago shook his head, simultaneously shaking the bottle. Two perfectly round holes in the plastic explained the lack of water: Someone had deliberately shot the jug to drain the water it held.

They kept going, their feet on autopilot, despite being tired of walking, tired of feeling their throats dry and sore, tired of traveling with no end in sight.

"You can eat cactus, right?" María Dolores stopped in front of a plant not much smaller than her.

Santiago grabbed her hand as she reached out toward the spiny arms as if hypnotized. "Not these ones. These don't have flesh or fruit. Just spines and wood-like bones inside. The eating ones are flat."

"Is it dinner time?" Alegría asked faintly from Santiago's neck.

The sound of her daughter perked up María Dolores. "Are you sure you can't eat these?"

Still holding María Dolores's hand, Santiago continued down the path. "Very sure. When I find a cactus we can eat, I'll give it to *ustedes*."

"Promise?"

"Of course."

The more they walked, the more his mind wandered. Where had all the cactus gone? Other people must have eaten them. He hated other people. He needed a stick to harvest the cactus. Or a fork to grab the pad. And a knife. He had a knife. That would help remove the spines. Or was it fire that removed the spines? He could make a fire.

Now the moon brought a chill, but the sun had burned like fire. Maybe the sun already burned off the spines. What spines?

After countless hours, the faded path ended at a road that stretched out to the left and right in the moonlight. Still a dirt road, but one wide enough for two cars to pass each other, evident by the tire tracks.

Here at the junction, instinct told Santiago to turn left. Left felt correct, left was farther away from the mountains they had crossed.

Behind him, María Dolores followed more slowly, her eyes on the road. When he remembered, he stopped and waited for her, shifting Alegría higher up on his hip.

So tired, too tired to think straight, and the empty backpack became too heavy to carry. He left that behind. But not Alegría. She stayed, now on his back, arms over his shoulders, legs crossed around his waist.

In the dark they didn't come across any cars. As the sun came up, vehicles started driving by. They couldn't risk being seen; *la migra* would just send them back. Santiago led them off the dirt road to walk in the brush instead, while keeping the road in sight as a guide. When a car came, they flattened themselves against the ground and hoped no one saw them. The third time they did this, Santiago didn't get up. The weight of Alegría on his back kept him pinned to the ground; he didn't have the strength to ask her to roll off. He turned his head. He could just make out María Dolores some distance behind him. She didn't move either.

A break. They could all use a break. Yes, just a little break.

CHAPTER 17

Lights flashed behind Santiago's eyelids. Pretty lights. Steady and consistent. Like a beating heart.

Except now his eyes were open. Red lights and blue lights. Warnings. Why would he see lights in the desert? And voices. Male voices. Maybe a female one too. But not María Dolores's voice. These voices didn't use words he understood.

"Santi." Alegría's voice came out breathless near his ear. Now that she spoke, he could feel her weight, comforting and close, still on his back. "Mami."

"Shh," he whispered. He forced his dehydrated mind to focus, comprehend the events in front of him, and stay hidden. Deep breaths: the only brain food available to him.

One set of flashing lights came from a police car. He

was pretty sure. The other from a large white van where a flat bed was being pulled out. A stretcher. An ambulance.

Two other cars were parked along the side. Lots of people talked. Still, none of the things they said made any sense. Not that it mattered. Police in any language didn't sound good.

"Shh," he reminded Alegría. He couldn't let the police notice them. *Stay hidden; don't let them see us.*

He noticed tangled bleached-blond hair mixed with black hair flutter against the desert ground. María Dolores.

Alegría whimpered in his ear. This time he didn't remind her to stay quiet.

People in uniforms lifted María Dolores onto the stretcher. The sight stung his eyes, but blinking hurt just as much; his body didn't have enough water to produce tears.

Her head rolled in their direction. The wind carried words from the scene he finally understood: "Alegr— San—."

The uniformed people shifted, blocking her from Santiago's sight. A male voice finally spoke in Spanish. "What are you saying? That you're *alegre*? Or are you praying to a saint?"

But no other words came from María Dolores.

Someone else gave an order, and the stretcher continued to the ambulance parked on the road.

The same person who'd spoken Spanish before changed

tactics. Instead of questioning, he turned to comforting. "You're safe. We're going to get you some water and food, and medical attention. You're going to be okay."

"Mami," Alegría sobbed against Santiago's shoulder as they loaded her *mamá* onto the ambulance twenty meters away.

He'd promised María Dolores he'd take care of Alegría. But he'd also promised himself he'd look after both of them. Yet here, now, in the desert, they were taking María Dolores away. Paramedics and police officers. Just like they'd taken his *mami* away.

He couldn't let them get caught. He had to save Alegría's life. Water. Food. He had none of those things. Didn't know where he could find them. But these people. They had water and food. Alegría needed water and food. Like she needed her *mami*.

The ambulance door slammed with a bang.

One hand held Alegría's leg to keep her steady. The other hand pressed against the ground, gathering his knees from under him, pushing and straining until he finally rolled up to standing. He raised the hand not supporting Alegría high into the air. *"Pare. ¡Alto!"*

CHAPTER 18

Santiago fell back to the ground as soon as the words crackled out of his throat. He heard the ambulance drive away; the people hadn't seen him. María Dolores. Lights and visions swam in and out of focus. No, he shouldn't have tried to get their attention. No, he shouldn't have let them get away.

Feet rushed to his side. Alegría's weight lifted from his back. No, not her, too. Fear fed anxiety as he struggled to his feet and stumbled forward onto his face.

"No . . . don't . . . her . . ." He struggled to talk, his throat too dry and his brain too fried. "Come. *Favor*. Not her."

The same male voice reassured him in Spanish. "She's right here. I'm giving her a drink. You drink too."

Strong hands rolled him over to his back and lifted his

head up, holding a drink to his lips. Except he couldn't. Not yet. Not until he knew for sure Alegría was okay.

"Santi." The figure who held out her hand looked nothing like Alegría. Most of the hair had come out of her pigtails, and it looked more like light brown instead of black. From mud? No, dust. There'd been no water to make mud. Her normally bright eyes were red and swollen. Her arms, which had been draped over his shoulders while he carried her, were burned past red and covered in blisters. Sunscreen. Hadn't they used sunscreen? Or had they eaten it? And when had they lost their hats? Days, weeks ago? His brain held no sense of time.

"Santi," she called out again after another swig from some yellow drink. At least she still sounded like her. "Where's Mami?"

Santiago took hold of the plastic bottle the man offered and swallowed most of it in one gulp. His stomach, the iron gut that could eat anything, revolted, and the yellow drink came right back up again.

"You have to take it slow. It'll help you. But slowly. A little at a time." The man tipped what felt like drops into Santiago's mouth. The sweetness clashed with the bile on his swollen tongue. His mouth absorbed that small amount without needing to swallow. A few more drops and, finally, one swallow made it down. Two more swallows and he reached his hand out to grab Alegría's.

"Where's Mami?" she repeated, her head turning from one side to the other.

Santiago squeezed her hand. Even with the minimal fluids, his brain regained some cognitive functions. And memory. The ambulance. And how once again he'd let paramedics take away his family.

"*Tu madre* is in need of critical care, suffering from extreme heatstroke," the man said. "They've taken her to the hospital. We didn't know you two were here until the ambulance left."

He wore a tan uniform that blended into the brown-and-tan landscape and a broad, flat-brimmed hat. By his dark eyes and wide nose, he could definitely be *mexicano*. His accent and manner of speaking, while flawless, indicated education, like a newscaster or politician.

"Come, let's get you out of the sun." He offered them each a hand, but neither accepted it. Instead, Santiago stood, lifted Alegría up, and then followed the tan-dressed man. His feet ached with every step, and the rest of his body felt stiff and brittle, like he'd snap if he weren't careful. Slower then, because he wouldn't let himself break, not while holding Alegría, not when he remained the only person she had left.

The truck had four doors and was the same tan color as the man's uniform. A design was printed on the back-seat door he opened for them. At least the truck didn't have flashing lights.

Despite the dark interior, the inside of the vehicle felt refreshingly cool. Santiago sank into the cushions, never wanting to get up, while Alegría remained clenched in a tight ball.

"Who are you?" Santiago asked.

"I'm Jorge, a ranger in these parts."

"*¿La migra?*"

"No, just a friend. Be right back. I have to finish talking with the others." The man left the car doors open and returned to the police officer and a woman standing by their nearby cars.

"I want my *mami!*" Alegría broke into tears and threw the drink bottle into the desert.

"*Mamita,*" Santiago said to the girl. He picked up the spilled drink and returned to the cool truck, reassuring himself as much as her. "We're going to see Mami real soon. Everything is all right. I'm here, and Princesa's here."

"Princesa is not real," Alegría muttered.

"*¿Qué?*" He leaned back to stare at the girl. The more he looked the more he could see the girl he remembered from before the sun had taken its toll on her face. He didn't want to think how he looked. "Of course Princesa is real. I see her; she's right in front of us. I think she's the one who got us help. I was really thirsty. Weren't you?"

She buried her face in his neck, nuzzling against him or maybe nodding yes.

He kissed her head and rubbed her back. "Whatever happens, we're both always here. Neither of us is going anywhere."

The policeman Jorge had been talking to barely looked their way as he got back into the squad car and turned off the flashing lights before driving away. Santiago let out a breath he hadn't known he was holding. One less thing to worry about.

The woman present wandered back to her car with her hands on her head and a look of disbelief. Once in the car, she didn't start it. Just rested her head on the steering wheel. She didn't wear a uniform.

Jorge returned and handed them each a plastic container of baby food and spoons. From the pictures, Santiago guessed it was some kind of meat (chicken?) and carrots.

"You probably won't be able to swallow anything more substantial for a while," Jorge explained. He turned the truck on and let the engine run with the air conditioner blasting but with the doors still open to the outside scorching world.

This Jorge didn't lock them in the truck. That said something. And the fact that he could waste money running the air conditioner with the doors open said something more. Maybe Jorge really was their friend.

"Here, *mamita*, you need to eat something." Santiago

opened the baby food and offered Alegría a spoonful. She shifted away from his neck and opened her mouth like a baby bird.

He scooped the next spoonful for himself. The baby food tasted bitter, like it'd been in the car for months, getting cooked by the intense heat. Alegría shook her head when he tried to offer her a second bite.

"You have to eat something. Build your strength so we can see Mami. Three more bites, okay?"

She responded by opening her mouth three more times, but no more. His own stomach agreed it'd had enough once they'd finished one container between the two of them.

"How did you find us?" Santiago asked as he drank more of the sweet yellow liquid.

"That woman over there thought she saw something this morning but didn't stop." He pointed to the woman in the other car, her head still on the steering wheel. "Later she saw it again and got out of the car. When she realized it was a person, she called for help. I think she's still in shock. We were just about to search the area for others when you stood up and fainted. Are there any others?"

"Other what?" Santiago asked.

"Other people traveling with you? Or anyone else you've seen?"

Santiago knew he should say they lived here, belonged

here. That their car had broken down and they'd gotten lost. But that would only bring questions he couldn't answer.

"There's no one else."

"Are you sure?" the man insisted. "The desert can take a life in a matter of hours. If there's anyone else out there, you'd be killing them by not letting me know—"

"It's just the three of us," Santiago confirmed. He didn't like these questions, like the man was trying too hard.

"You're lucky we found you when we did. I don't think you would have made it the rest of the day."

"Will Ma—my sister be okay?"

"Too soon to tell."

Santiago's head wobbled, and his eyes began to droop. Already Alegría was sound asleep with her head against his shoulder. He could feel the drool through his shirt. Good, a sign of rehydration. He yawned.

The truck began to move. Deep in his brain, something called for caution. Of what? Or why? Except his brain had already proceeded to go into hibernation. It had been given fluids, food, and a cool environment. Not as much as it needed, but enough to let his guard down.

CHAPTER 19

A hand shaking his shoulder woke Santiago up. Outside, the sunset lit the vast landscape of nothingness: scrawny, shade-less bushes; spiny, inedible cacti; and a distant mountain range that had only led to disappointment. He couldn't tell if they'd crossed the border again and been sent back.

The tan truck sat in a parking lot surrounded by a tall chain-link fence topped with razor wire. A gray building loomed in front of him. The two flags, one with stars and stripes and the other with a golden sun, waving high above the entrance confirmed they weren't in México.

Why did he get the feeling he and Alegría were being sent to jail? Or was that just how hospitals looked over here?

"What's happening? Is María Dolores here?" Santiago asked. Panic rose inside. He had to get them out. Away from the danger. But their rescuer blocked the open door.

"No, she'll stay in the hospital for a while. She suffered from much more extreme heatstroke than you did. Her condition is still critical."

"So why are we here?" Santiago held tight to Alegría's hand.

Jorge leaned against the doorframe. "You're kids without an adult in our country illegally. They'll take care of you until your situation is reviewed."

What situation? Santiago could take care of himself, and Alegría. He didn't need adult supervision. Especially not in this place that resembled a prison. "How long? Until María Dolores gets out of the hospital?"

"I honestly don't know. It varies. *Vamos*. We have to go in." Jorge shifted aside to let them out.

Santiago didn't move except to look at Alegría, the girl he'd promised to take care of. "There has to be another way."

"Sure." Jorge shrugged. "I drive you back to México, and you can see how the police down there treat you."

No police, no going back. Not just for himself, he couldn't do that to Alegría.

"Of course, if you return to México," Jorge continued, "your sister might never find you."

They'd been played. Presenting an option ten times worse than the original one to cover the fact that there wasn't really an option. Being admitted into this facility was inevitable.

Santiago slid out of the car before grasping Alegría in his arms. Jorge led them forward with a hand on Santiago's shoulder. So much for being a friend.

"How's Princesa doing?" Santiago asked Alegría in a falsely cheerful whisper.

"I don't know—she's missing." She said the words, but they didn't surprise him. Somehow he'd known that this place barred all invisible entities.

"She'll come back. But until she does, we need to be brave."

Three wide steps led to glass doors at the entrance to the facility. Jorge's hand dropped from Santiago's shoulder to press a button in the wall and speak into the receiver in English.

Panic and adrenaline fused with minimal nourishment fueled his desperation. *Now, go!* Santiago leaped down the three steps like a colt on a racetrack, clutching Alegría to his chest for dear life. His vision blurred, but he didn't slow his pace, blinking hard, forcing himself to keep going. One last chance.

"*¡Alé, alé!*" Alegría's cheers encouraged him to stretch his legs and run faster. He wove through the vehicles, heading for the open gates.

He could do it. They could do it! The open gates had to be a sign. Of possibilities, of freedom.

Except the gates began to close. It had to be a trick, a hallucination. Another effect of his tired and starving body. No trick. Just as he reached the gates, they clanged shut.

He rammed his shoulder against the metal gate before slowly crumpling to the ground with his back against it. Alegría unwound her legs from his waist and curled up in his lap instead. Gasping for breath, he banged the back of his head against the fence a few times. He should have run for it as soon as Jorge opened the truck door. They would have made it then.

Stupid, stupid. His heart pounded as if any minute it would break free from his body.

Their escort took his time ambling back to them, hands in the pockets of his tan uniform pants. When Jorge reached them, he offered his hand like he'd done when he first found them alongside the road.

Alegría shifted to sit squarely on Santiago's lap, faced Jorge, and placed her hands on her hips. A rumble came from somewhere. It took a second for Santiago to recognize it as a growl. Coming from Alegría.

"Let us go," she demanded.

"You know that's not happening. You either come willingly, get some more food and water, or I call two guys to pry you apart and take you both in *a toda fuerza*. Your choice."

Alegría reached behind her back and pulled Santiago's arms to wrap around her. They stayed like that for a few minutes until Santiago, his breath still not fully returned, let out a deep sigh.

"*Mamita*, I don't know what else to do."

She dropped her defiant act and turned to curl up against his chest. She'd tried to save him. No one had ever stood up for him like that. He pressed his head against hers, taking in the last lingering scent of her fruity shampoo.

Slowly, carefully, he eased himself up while his arms stayed wrapped tightly around her. Jorge fell in step with them, this time gripping Santiago's bicep as they walked back to the reflective doors.

Before getting to the door, Santiago looked over his shoulder, just once, to make sure the gates were still shut.

They were.

Inside, a woman dressed in a blue uniform asked for their names and country of birth.

With no proof, they couldn't lie and say they were born in Los Estados Unidos. Plus, it would make it harder to be reunited with María Dolores. Their stories had to match. "Santiago García Reyes, and this is Alegría García Piedra. We're Mexican. She's my sister."

María Dolores would definitely declare him as a brother.

Most likely.

Hopefully.

The officer demanded that they place their fingertips on some kind of screen. A light lit up, scanning their fingerprints. Like they were criminals.

A different officer then waved them through the metal detector, which beeped. They confiscated Santiago's pocketknife, lighter, and peso coin Domínguez had given him. It wasn't until this point that Santiago noticed that Jorge had completely vanished.

Once clear of the metal detector, they were escorted into a white room with bright fluorescent lights and several folding chairs. Four other people inhabited the room with them: a teenage girl with her arms crossed over her chest and face hidden in her sweatshirt hood, a boy older than Alegría hiding underneath two chairs and sucking his thumb, another boy curled up across three of the chairs with his back to them as he tried to sleep, and a guard who occasionally looked up from his newspaper. On one side, the combined man/woman stick figures indicated a bathroom next to a water fountain. Besides the solid door they'd come through, another door stood at the opposite end of the room with a small window that had veins going through the glass in diamond shapes.

Santiago set Alegría down in front of the water fountain. "Drink a little at a time. We don't want to get sick."

Every few minutes they got up from their chairs for another sip of water. It gave Santiago something to do. It also helped to fill their bellies, which moaned with hunger.

Soon Alegría tugged his sleeve. "I have to go *pipí*."

"It's there." He pointed.

"Come with me."

He understood. He didn't want to let her out of his sight either, though he doubted the bathroom had additional exits. He opened the door for her, and they slipped in just as the guard called out in Spanish, "Only one person allowed at a time."

Santiago pretended not to hear him and closed the door behind them. "Go ahead. I won't look."

The room consisted of one toilet and sink, and a mirror he avoided. He splashed cool water on his face, which stung against his sunburned flesh. Brown-and-red water whirled around the white sink before draining.

Once the toilet flushed, he changed places with Alegría.

"Wash your hands with soap. If you put water on your face, it both hurts and feels good." He positioned himself to the side of the toilet so his back remained to her. Peeing stung worse than washing his face had, and it came out almost brown. There was also the feeling of not being able to get it all out. Like in a few minutes he'd need to go again.

The whole front of Alegría's shirt displayed a much darker color than normal, and the floor near the sink resembled a small pond. His own shirt also sported a wet bib. For a quick second he thought of cleaning up the mess after them, then decided against it.

"Next time, only one person is allowed in the bathroom at a time," the guard repeated as they exited.

Santiago gave him a noncommittal nod.

Upon their return to the holding room, the little boy who'd been under the chairs had left. The girl in the hoodie went through the windowed door next. A new boy, this one more man than kid with his mustache and tattooed muscles, entered through the admittance door. He did nothing but rest his chin in his hands, but with this new guy present, the guard looked up from his newspaper more often.

The guards rotated before the next person got called through the windowed door. This guard stood against the wall with arms larger than Santiago's body crossed over his chest. Santiago could feel his eyes on him every time he and Alegría went to the water fountain.

Santiago turned his back to the guard, desperate for the "out of sight, out of mind" relief. The hairs on his sunburned neck said the guard maintained surveillance on him. A camera like a black eye hanging from the ceiling watched them as well.

Ignore them and they'll ignore you.

He undid Alegría's messy pigtails. Using his fingers as a comb, he carefully untangled every knot that had made her head look more like a rat's nest than hair.

"Tell me a story, Santi," she whispered.

As his fingers worked, he told her one he'd heard many times at her age about a princess who stood up to the wind spirit to save her people. "And she told the wind that she belonged with her people and her people belonged with her, and no distance would change that," Santiago concluded.

"So she saved the villagers?" Alegría asked as he gently arranged her hair back into two smooth, though still dusty, pigtails.

"Of course. Because good, brave princesses who love their people are stronger than any spirit that tries to harm them."

An officer, different from the one who had checked them in, entered the room through the windowed door.

"Alegría García Piedra," she said.

Santiago stood up, holding the little girl's hand. Together they approached the officer.

She shook her head. "No. *Solo la niña.*"

Her Spanish wasn't very good, her accent so strong, Santiago figured she must have used the wrong words by mistake. "I'm her brother. We go together."

Again the officer shook her head. "She needs bath and see female doctor. You not female."

His grip on Alegría's hand tightened. That sounded like an excuse rather than the truth. "I don't mind if a female doctor looks me over."

"No, they are the rules."

He lifted Alegría back into his arms. "I'm not leaving her. Her *mamá* is in the hospital. I'm the only person she has. She's the only person I have."

A slight head tilt made it look like the officer had agreed to let them go as a unit. Santiago stepped closer to the windowed door. Except two big arms grabbed him from behind, wrenching loose Santiago's hold on Alegría. The officer broke Alegría's grip from around his neck, causing him to choke as she accidentally pressed against his throat.

"Santi!" Alegría called out as her legs kicked at the officer behind her.

"Alegría!" Santiago lunged toward her, but the grip on him didn't loosen. The male guard lifted Santiago off his feet like a rag doll and pulled him away just as the female officer did the same with Alegría.

"Please, she's my sister. Alegría!" he choked out, the guard's muscles crushing his body.

"Santi!" she called one last time before they passed through the heavy, windowed door. It clicked shut without another sound.

PART 2

CHAPTER 20

Youth immigration center

Out of spite—Santiago was sure of it—they kept him in the waiting room longer than anyone else. Even another new boy was brought in and called immediately.

That's what he got for spending an hour screaming for Alegría after she was taken away. He stopped only when his throat became so raw, he could no longer make a sound. He even dared to look through the foreboding window but only saw a corridor. When he tested the door handle, it turned but didn't open.

Finally, exhausted, he hugged his knees to his chest and rocked back and forth on the folding chair, wide eyes staring at the door that took people away but didn't bring them back.

Another guard changed places with the awful, burly one. Except this one smelled of roasted meat and seasoned vegetables. Santiago's stomach rumbled as he drank more water to stifle the hunger. Honestly, he didn't know which guard he hated more.

It felt like days before Santiago finally heard his name called. He jumped to his feet and rushed to the door. Alegría must be so worried. But he'd be with her soon. He'd make sure she never had to worry again.

His escort couldn't have been much older than himself, with a face full of pimples and a head of greasy, black hair. He led Santiago down the corridor and opened a door to a shower room.

"Take off all your clothes and make sure to wash every single part of your body—hair, armpits, privates, feet. There's soap on the wall." His Spanish sounded Mexican, and Santiago couldn't help feeling betrayed: This guard was turning his back on his own people by working in this facility.

A curtain offered some privacy, but the guard's looming presence behind it did nothing to reassure Santiago. Still, he did as he was told, the tepid water stinging his sunburned flesh. Dirt encrusted his scalp, and even with his very short hair, it took two scrubbing sessions for the water from his head to run clean. While he washed the rest of his body, the contrast between his arm and his stomach shocked him—almost black compared to the light brown it should be. He shut the water off quickly, not wanting to see more.

The guard handed him a towel and a pair of flip-flops. Santiago's clothes and shoes had magically disappeared. A sinking feeling suggested he'd never see them again. The last link to María Dolores, gone.

Still dripping, he was directed into a room with an ominous-looking chair. Strange machines hummed and blinked as if communicating with the other occupant of the room: an older white man with white hair and a white mustache wearing a white coat. But with red eyes, as if he hadn't slept in days.

The man spoke to him in English. When Santiago didn't move, the man motioned him to remove the towel. Santiago trembled, not just from the cold temperature. Fear rattled his bones more than ever since arriving at the facility, such fear not felt since he'd last been at *la malvada*'s house. Every time the man approached him, he cowered; every time he was touched, he flinched. No one had ever examined him before.

But nothing bad really happened. The man placed cold instruments on his body or in his mouth for a few moments and then removed them. A slight prick in one arm withdrew blood, and a few different pricks in the other arm injected stuff into his body.

Finally the doctor handed him a salve and indicated that Santiago should rub it on his face, arms, and neck. Instant relief came to his sun-fried skin, and he liberally rubbed more on. The doctor motioned Santiago to wrap himself in the towel again and ushered him out the door.

"You get clean clothes three times a week," said the pimply guard waiting for him with a fresh pile of clothes. The mound of cotton and polyester weighed down his arms. Would he stay long enough to need new ones? White underwear and socks, gray drawstring sweatpants, gray long-sleeve shirt, and gray sweatshirt. The flip-flops apparently were the only accepted footwear.

Once Santiago was dressed (the guard had to get him smaller underwear), they arrived at their final destination: a packed and partially lit room, where the temperature felt near freezing. The guard handed him a toothbrush wrapped in plastic and a large metallic thing that crinkled like aluminum foil. Judging by the shiny sleeping bodies clumped around the bare floor, the thing was apparently some kind of blanket. So strange that a sheet like that was expected to provide warmth. Instead, his eyes searched for two pigtails, or maybe just shoulder-length dark hair, now clean and splayed across the floor.

Except all of the ninety-some bodies were too big to be Alegría. Even in the low light, a second glance confirmed that not only were they all teenagers, they were also all boys.

CHAPTER 21

"Where's Alegría? Where are the girls?" Santiago demanded.

But the pimply guard gave him a severe shushing, and some of the guys turned in their sleep. Another guard, this one bald and with a big belly, walked over to them and pointed to a microscopic vacancy on the crowded floor.

"Please, my sister. Where is she? Is she okay?" Santiago whispered.

"All the girls sleep in a different area," the bald guard whispered back. "For their safety."

Their safety? But it was *his* job to keep Alegría safe. "Please, just tell me she's okay."

The guards ignored him and once again pointed to the floor.

Too tired to complain further, knowing he'd get nowhere with these guys tonight, he wove his way through the sleeping bodies and plopped down at "his" spot. From tiredness or hunger, his brain turned off before he finished pulling the metallic sheet over his legs.

The blaring alarm, after what felt like seconds later, caused Santiago to jump to his feet. Heart pounding, ears ringing, Santiago took in the teenage boys waking up—some joking with one another, some cursing at the stupid early wake-up call—and crumpled back to the floor.

All around him were gray teenagers and gray walls. Fluorescent lights overhead and no windows. A few closed doors lined one of the walls; the one open door emitted sounds from a television. Half of the guys lined up for the bathroom. The exit, noticeable by its steel door, required a guard's key card to open.

The pimply guard, still on duty, came by and kicked him in the leg. Not hard enough to hurt, but still a kick. "*Levántate*. Get up."

Santiago scrambled to his feet, still clutching the metallic blanket. He wouldn't cry.

Little kids he understood. Adults, he knew more or less how to act around them. But this in-between bunch, his peers, presented a completely alien species. His older cousins never played with him, never wanted him around. And friends . . . He never stayed in one location long enough to hang out with anyone, and no one had bothered to send him to school.

He knew enough about teenage boys, however, not to break down crying. It would take every bit of willpower not to, but he could do it. He'd have to stay strong. For Alegría.

He draped his metallic blanket over his arm—somehow, the flimsy sheet had kept him warm in the freezing room during the night—and took a deep breath before approaching a different guard on duty.

"Excuse me, when can I see my sister?"

This guard, red faced with blond hair, shook his head.

"*Mi hermana,*" Santiago repeated. He tapped his chest for "my." For "sister" he held his hand at her height and then mimed pigtails against his head. "*¿Dónde está?*"

The guard shrugged and said something in English that Santiago didn't understand.

"You're not going to get anything out of him, *bróder,*" a guy with a strange accent called out. Santiago turned. A long scar ran down the side of his face, reflected for a second by the folded metallic sheet before he stuffed it into his pocket.

"*Este tipo,*"—he motioned at the guard—"doesn't know a drop of Spanish. Or at least pretends not to. You're wasting your time talking to him."

Once again Santiago noticed his *acento* and the usage

of words he hadn't heard before. He understood them in context but had never heard the use of *vos* instead of *tú*. At least it sounded friendly.

"*Sabe usted* who I can ask about my sister and when I can see her?" Santiago used the formal form for "you," a term reserved for older people or those he wished to respect. Yes, that made him a kiss-up, but if it meant getting answers, he'd be overly polite to anyone who might help.

Acento shook his head just as the guard had. "You won't. Not in here. You won't see her, and the guards won't tell you anything about her. They say it's to keep people safe. Personally, I think it's to hold power. Only bullies separate you from your family."

The shiny blanket slipped from Santiago's arm. He couldn't see Alegría. His broken promise to keep her safe lay crumpled on the floor like the flimsy sheet. Still, he wouldn't cry. "*¿Tiene usted hermanos aquí también?*"

"Please, you don't have to keep using *usted* with me. I'm only eighteen, not that old." Acento grinned a smile of white, even teeth to lighten the mood but then turned serious again. "No, I don't have any siblings, but I've been here a long time. Long enough to know how things work. You won't see your sister again until you get out."

Though he didn't say it, the looming *if you get out* seemed implied.

So this was jail. No one told him this would happen

if he came to *el otro lado*, but no one told him much of anything.

"And parents?" Santiago asked.

Acento pressed his lips together and averted his eyes. "This is a youth facility, and we're divided by age and gender—no grown-ups live here. I don't know of any kid who's been given visitation rights to see anyone. Maybe the girls' side is different."

Again, the words he didn't say held more meaning: He didn't think the girls had different rules. Which meant if María Dolores was alive and left the hospital, she'd be taken someplace else, and Alegría might never see her again. If anything happened to Alegría . . .

Except he would never know.

"I feel sick." Santiago rubbed his head. What if Alegría were sick too? They were probably feeling the similar effects of heat exhaustion.

Acento placed a cool hand on Santiago's sunburned forehead and stared at him with intense green eyes. "You have a fever. And you look hungry. Did you get any food when you arrived?"

"Nothing."

"Stupid, inhumane, privileged scumbags," Acento muttered. "At least breakfast is in a half hour. You'll feel better once you've eaten." He nodded toward the metallic sheet Santiago had dropped. "You don't have to, but I suggest you fold your blanket and keep it in your pocket. That way you're not stuck with a torn one come bedtime—they're not replaced regularly. Pocket your toothbrush as well and anything else you want to keep safe, or someone will steal it."

Santiago nodded his thanks and understanding, though he didn't know what else he would want to secure. The pocketknife and lighter had been taken away from him, and the backpack had been lost somewhere in the desert.

"Is this why they give us these things instead of real blankets?" Santiago forced himself to make small talk as he folded it. "Because they don't take up much space?"

Acento grinned. "That's the most realistic reason I've heard yet. Some guys have the theory that they can be used as communication devices—they haven't succeeded yet. They're really for vermin and disease control. Real blankets are always infested with so many people coming in and out."

That made sense. Santiago's Tía Roberta had had him boil his cousins' clothes after their lice epidemic. "So we're stuck with aluminum foil."

"And why the temperature is kept really low."

They joined the other boys lining up for the bathroom.

"So, do you have a name?" The words Acento said were almost exactly as María Dolores had said them when he first met her all that time ago, except Acento again used *vos* instead of *tú*.

"Yeah, it's Santi." He'd never asked anyone to call him that before, but it reminded him of Alegría, keeping her close by. "How about you?"

"In here they call me Guanaco."

Ah, that explained the strange accent; he came from El Salvador. "But isn't that an offensive term?"

"*Ey,*" the Salvadoran admitted. "The guy who started calling me that certainly meant to insult me. But it's only insulting if I let it be. So instead, I'm owning it. I'm proud of who I am."

"I've never been proud of who I am." The words came out of Santiago's mouth before he could stop them.

Guanaco turned and looked hard at Santiago. "Then maybe you should change that. Be someone worth being proud of."

María Dolores had told him something like that too.

"Even in here?" Santiago gestured to the four gray walls that separated them from their families, as if they were no better than criminals.

Guanaco moved forward a few paces in the bathroom line, his green eyes fixed on Santiago. "Especially in here."

The bathroom they entered had five urinals, five stalls, five sinks, and five showers along with one guard sitting in a chair near the sinks.

"Is there always someone in here?" Santiago whispered into Guanaco's ear.

The older guy gave him a slow nod. "Always. Even if you come in at night, one of the night guards follows you in. A few months ago, some guys beat up another kid in one of the showers. The guards tried restricting bathroom usage, but then people kept peeing wherever they felt like it. So now we have a monitor."

"We never get any privacy?"

"Nowhere's private here. You're always being watched."

Guanaco entered a free stall. The urinal closest to the guard became available, but Santiago waved the next boy over to use it. Normally he wouldn't think twice that someone could be watching him, but the fact that the bathroom needed a guard to be safe made him feel vulnerable and uneasy.

When a stall became free, he entered and leaned his head against the wall behind the toilet. Two fat tears rolled down his cheeks. He couldn't do this. This staying here, not knowing anything. Never before did he want information so badly. What could he do to learn something about Alegría? To get them both out? From what he could tell, nothing.

He dabbed his eyes with toilet paper, careful not to rub them or they'd turn red and indicate to the world he'd been crying. He did his business and then washed his hands with soap before splashing cold water on his face. To anyone watching, it'd look like he used that method to wake up.

Guanaco waited for him outside the bathroom with two freshly showered friends, making no comment about the length of time Santiago had spent in the bathroom.

"This is Pinocchio." Guanaco introduced him to a boy with a large, beaklike nose and then gestured to the other, who wore thick glasses. "And Mosca."

"Do you have any family outside?" Pinocchio asked as they got in line for breakfast.

"*Sí*," Santiago lied without thinking about it.

"Lucky," Guanaco said. "It's people like me who have no one that they don't know what to do with."

His words circled in Santiago's brain. He didn't really have family outside of the facility. Not with María Dolores dead or heading for a detention center herself; he'd never met her sister, María Eugenia, and didn't know where she lived. Maybe last night they hadn't kept him waiting so long as punishment. Maybe they already didn't know what to do with him. Just like living with *la malvada*: he was the parasite no one could get rid of.

"So they'll send you back?" Santiago asked.

Guanaco shrugged. "I hope not, but I've been here for over five months, and I've just turned eighteen. They won't keep me much longer. I don't know if they'll send me to an adult facility or not. My parents were murdered in El Salvador; I got attacked and held for ransom in México before escaping." He pointed to the scar down his otherwise handsome face. "I came to the border seeking asylum. Supposedly that's one of the correct ways of entering the country, instead of overstaying your visit or sneaking in. They don't like it when you do that."

Sneaking in. Just as he and María Dolores had done. The possibility of doing it the "correct way" hadn't even crossed his mind, not that he understood what classified as "correct." Guanaco said he'd followed the rules and still ended up in this center. In that case, how could anyone know what was right? No one, not *la migra* or anyone else working in their government seemed to know the rules anyway.

"I hope they grant you asylum," Santiago said.

"Thanks, *bróder*." Guanaco patted him on the back. "I wish you luck too."

A guard in the front and another bringing up the rear escorted them out of the main area and into the locked hallway Santiago had been through last night. Single file, half a meter apart, arms behind their backs, absolutely no touching. When one of the boys said he wasn't hungry, the guards forced him to join the line anyway. Santiago frantically sought a glimpse of the girls in the maze of corridors but saw no one. They arrived in the cafeteria, which, according to Mosca, "served *medio mundo*" before the teenage boys finally got to eat.

Breakfast consisted of milk with dry cereal and fruit.

Santiago started filling up one bowl of something colorful, but both Pinocchio and Mosca loaded *two* bowls with cereal. His stomach rumbled, but he remembered how his body had rejected food yesterday.

"How many meals do we get in here?" he asked.

"Three. There's usually not enough, so grab what you can." Mosca spoke in a Guatemalan accent.

"And when there is enough, it's because no one else wants it," Pinocchio added in his Mexican accent. "Just don't try to sneak food out of the cafeteria. We get searched before leaving to prevent that."

Twelve boys stood in line behind Santiago. There should still be enough for them if he took both the colorful cereal and the healthier-looking brown one.

"Grab two oranges as well." Guanaco motioned to the fruit.

Santiago's hand had already been reaching for one. "Two?"

Guanaco picked off the smallest bit of the orange peel to show him the white interior. "Yeah, and eat this white bit too. It'll boost your immune system. You need all the vitamins you can get. This isn't a place to get sick. Two of the little kids have been taken to the hospital. They tried to hide it from us, but we all saw the ambulance arrive."

Santiago followed them to the long, sticky tables with benches attached at either side. The other boys talked while he ate his first meal in a long time. He only managed part of the colorful bowl of cereal before he started feeling nauseous. Maybe sugary cereal hadn't been the best choice for his first meal, no matter how pretty and tasty. He couldn't even look at the brown cereal now congealed into mush. His eyes shut as he brought an orange to his nose to ease his stomach.

Guanaco placed a hand on his shoulder. "It happens to everyone, but you'll get used to it. On Sundays we get eggs from a box and sausages that have sent many a good man straight to the toilets."

Mosca groaned in agreement.

Santiago opened one eye while keeping the orange against his nose. "How can eggs come from a box?"

"No clue, *bróder*, but trust me—they do." Guanaco grimaced.

Santiago lowered the orange and opened both eyes. He waited a few seconds to make sure he could talk. "Why are you telling me all this? Why are you helping me? You don't know me."

"Maybe not you exactly, but I know what you're going through." The sad look returned to his green eyes. "I've been separated from someone I care about too. Not a sister, but a girlfriend. While crossing México. I don't know where she is, if she's even alive. But at least I know she hasn't come through this facility."

"How do you know that?" So there *was* a way to get information about the girls.

Guanaco and his two friends stood up to return their food trays. "It's a feeling I have in my heart. I just know."

Santiago stayed seated with his food a bit longer—the guard said they had two minutes left. A middle-aged woman wearing an apron and a hairnet came out to collect the trays. She kept her head down, and as a result, everyone ignored her. A plan began to form in his mind. Santiago took two more bites of his cereal and brought his tray to her cart.

"Thank you for the food," he whispered, knowing they'd get into trouble for talking.

Her head jerked up in surprise. Then she whispered back, *"De nada."*

CHAPTER 22

Santiago lay staring at the industrial gray ceiling with his metallic blanket over his body and his arms tucked behind his head for a pillow. The concrete floor pressed hard and cold against his back. The lights overhead dimmed but were still bright enough to illuminate the sleeping figures around him. Pinocchio and Mosca whispered on the other side of Guanaco. Some boys curled up in the fetal position, clutching tight to the collar of their sweatshirts while trying to hide the fact that they were crying. Others shifted every few seconds, the rustle of their metallic blankets giving away their desperation to find that one spot that was slightly less uncomfortable than the others.

The lack of a bed didn't bother him—that was how he'd slept most nights of his life. Sometimes with a ratty blanket, sometimes not even that. Even the lights weren't what kept him awake. He could sleep through anything, and had: shouting, bangs, fires. No, the physical discomforts were hardly noticeable compared to the thoughts running through his mind. Too drained to join the undercover fetal weepers, he just stared straight up at the lights.

Guanaco, he noticed, lay perfectly still next to him. Too still to be asleep. The four of them had secured a corner, prime real estate compared to camping out in the middle of the room. The secret, Guanaco had explained, was to get there first. Despite what they called this place, a temporary immigration holding facility or whatever, Santiago felt sentenced to jail.

And he'd allowed Alegría to be sentenced here too. No wonder he couldn't sleep.

He shifted to his side with a loud rustle, almost hugging the wall with an arm horizontal against the concrete. He remembered that last day in the desert (was that only yesterday?) with Alegría's weight against his back. Even in his tired and dehydrated state, just feeling her presence had brought comfort. With some imagination, he could feel her warmth and pulse as if she were next to him now, just on the other side of the wall.

The fantasy relaxed his mind. Maybe he'd eventually fall asleep. Even with the hard floor, illuminated room, and continual twittering of almost a hundred teenagers.

Except someone let out a loud fart amplified by the high ceiling. Silence fell for a few seconds before a suppressed giggle echoed through the room. Then another, and another, before full-blown laughter erupted from all sides. A snicker escaped Santiago's own lips. He couldn't help it.

"Shh," one of the night guards reprimanded.

The silence lasted less than a second before someone forced a huge burp, which led to an even louder burst of laughter. Another person burped, and someone else responded with an armpit noise.

"*¡Cállense!*" the guard shouted.

A chorus of bodily noises continued whenever silence lasted for more than a second. Santiago turned to his stomach and hid his head under the metallic blanket and under his arms. Still, he could hear the guards going around, shushing and kicking people to be quiet.

"Don't the guards know they'll stop if they're ignored?" Santiago mumbled to himself. His little cousins had always misbehaved more when they had an audience.

"At least they're not barking," Guanaco muttered back. "The night that happened, they even got the coyotes outside to howl back."

"Is falling asleep ever easy here?" Santiago lifted his head from the floor and turned to face the wall.

A slight rustling indicated Guanaco shaking his head. "Not as long as I've been here."

CHAPTER 23

On Santiago's second day a kid started screaming as soon as the guard delivered him into the crowded room. "Where are the phones? Don't I get a phone call?"

The red-faced guard on duty was the one who didn't know, or pretended not to know, Spanish. Patterson, as Santiago heard others call him, had a special talent for ignoring anyone other than a fellow guard.

Just as he'd helped Santiago, Guanaco set the newcomer straight. "Sorry, *bróder*, phone calls don't happen here. We have fewer rights than murderers."

"But no one knows I'm here. How will I get rescued?"

"Grow out your hair," Pinocchio muttered under his breath. "Get a spoon and start digging."

Guanaco narrowed his eyes at his friend before turning

back to the newcomer. "You'll get an intake interview in a couple days, *brodér*. There you give them the contact information, and they'll let your family know you're here."

Sure, that all sounded fine. Except Santiago didn't know how to contact María Dolores or how to find out if she was even alive. More pressing would be getting a message to Alegría. Their caravans to the cafeteria and the outside area were carefully timed so they never crossed paths with the other youths at the center who shared the same amenities (though some of the boys swore they had caught glimpses of the teenage girls a couple of times). This morning, for the briefest second, Santiago heard someone crying as his group filed toward breakfast. A reminder they weren't alone. Somewhere within the gray walls of this building, Alegría waited for him. Now to figure out how to get in touch with her.

Santiago kept his head down and scuffed the hard dirt with the toe of his flip-flop. Sometimes once, sometimes twice a day they got to spend time outside in the "play" area—nothing more than a bare patch of earth surrounded by a tall chain-link fence topped with razor wire. No balls, and running around was only allowed while certain guards were on duty. But just like the cafeteria, this area was also used by the younger boys and the girls—a broken plastic barrette found in the dirt proved that. If he could only write Alegría's name in the dirt, would she see it before someone stepped on it? Would she know it came from him and he meant to say he missed her and thought of her all the time? A long shot he'd be willing to risk.

He'd just have to learn to write.

"*Oye*, Guanaco, I got something for you." A boy of about fourteen, shorter than Santiago but with broad shoulders, strutted up to them.

"Not interested, Chismoso," the older boy said as he did a series of jumping jacks while his friends talked with some other guys.

Chismoso leaned against the chain-link fence. "You don't know what it is."

"Don't want to." Guanaco continued with his jumping jacks.

From his accent, the other boy sounded Mexican, but Santiago couldn't say from what part. "Your days here are numbered, my friend."

"I knew that from the start."

Santiago heard Guanaco's formal tone, saw the narrowing of his eyes at being called "friend."

Chismoso shrugged and strutted away. He hadn't gone too far when he called out to another boy. "*Mira, burro*, we're having spaghetti tonight. Pay up."

Secret messages in the hard dirt temporarily forgotten,

Santiago moved closer to Guanaco, who'd stopped his exercise.

"Is Chismoso really his name?" Santiago asked.

Guanaco shrugged. "It's what we call him."

The fact that Chismoso's nickname meant "gossiper" shouldn't have surprised Santiago.

"What things does he know?" Santiago asked as a thought brewed.

"Many. And they're usually true." Guanaco laced his fingers through the fence and leaned into his muscular shoulders to stretch his back. "But finding out comes at a price. I won't deal with him. Don't like being indebted to anyone."

Santiago couldn't drop it. "If I want to find out how my sister is doing, Chismoso could do that?"

"That's a reasonable assumption." Guanaco turned his back to him.

Santiago heard the disapproval. "You don't want me to talk to him."

This time Guanaco faced him. Despite the age difference, they were almost the same height. "No, *bróder*, I'm not saying that. People have to make their own choices."

Santiago glanced at Chismoso, still talking with the guy he'd called Burro, a nickname that kid surely hadn't given himself. "Chismoso's the one who started calling you Guanaco, isn't he?"

"Ten other guys were here from El Salvador when I arrived, but yes, I'm the one who got the ethnic slur."

What name would this gossiper give Santiago? It would be something Santiago wouldn't like. Except Chismoso wouldn't know there were few things that Santiago hadn't been called already.

Santiago's voice softened in sympathy. "Can you do me a favor?"

But Guanaco shook his head. "I don't run that kind of operation."

"It's only"—Santiago shuffled a flip-flop back and forth—"to ask if you can write my sister's name here in the dirt? Maybe she'll see it and know I'm thinking about her."

Guanaco's face relaxed into a smile. "Yeah, okay, I can do that."

"Gracias." And even though he didn't know what the word meant, he added, *"Bróder."*

"Alfaro!" Patterson, the guard who never spoke to the inhabitants, called across the yard.

Guanaco straightened up his shoulders and let out a deep breath. The other ninety or hundred teens outside stopped their chitchat and games. The smug look on Chismoso's face screamed, *I told you so.*

A crowd formed a few meters behind Guanaco as he headed toward Patterson.

"*¿Voy a salir?*" Guanaco asked the guard, and then switched to English. "I'm free?"

But Patterson just jerked his head toward the door in response.

The muscles around Santiago's face twitched. Guanaco was leaving. Santiago wished Guanaco could stay or, better yet, that he could go with him. He swallowed and offered the older boy a hand; Guanaco shook it.

"No touching!" Patterson yelled in English. Not knowing what that meant, Santiago dropped Guanaco's hand.

"I hope you find your girlfriend," Santiago whispered.

"Me too." Guanaco's regular confidence faltered. He turned and waved at Pinocchio, Mosca, and all the other boys, giving them a smile that didn't reach his green eyes.

Santiago swallowed harder this time, watching his only friend follow the guard out. Whatever decision the government made for Guanaco, Santiago hoped it'd be a favorable one.

CHAPTER 24

Once Guanaco left, Santiago kept to himself. Pinocchio and Mosca let him sit next to them during meals, but Santiago declined. He didn't have anything to say to them. He still didn't know how to talk to kids his own age. Besides, eating alone gave him a chance to plan.

When the guards called time, some of the boys left their food trays on the long tables. It took Santiago a few extra seconds to pile the remaining trays and take the stack where it belonged. Not too different from what he'd done in Capaz. The second time Santiago did this, the lady who came out at the end of the mealtimes to clean up accepted the trays from his arms.

"No tiene que hacer eso." She whispered her gratitude with respect.

"Ya sé," Santiago whispered back. Except he did have to help her.

During an evening meal, he introduced himself as he threw away wrappers that had fallen next to the trash. *"Soy Santiago."*

"Y yo Consuelo."

He wanted to say something more, but Patterson yelled at him to stop wasting time and get in line to return to the main room. That much English he'd learned.

The next day at breakfast, as soon as Consuelo came out, he took his bowl of milky cereal debris and orange peels to the trash. Except he "accidentally" tripped on his flip-flops, spilling cereal mush all over the floor.

"¡Ay, perdóneme!" he apologized, then grabbed a couple of napkins to help Consuelo clean up the mess. Their heads together, he whispered, "Can you find out about my sister, Alegría? She's five and wears pigtails."

Of course, María Dolores had styled her hair like that. He couldn't imagine a guard doing that here.

"I'll ask around," Consuelo murmured without hesitation. "Do you want me to give her something?"

Something? What could he give her? All he had was a toothbrush and a metallic blanket; all that remained in the dining room were spilled food and trays. He glanced at the guards. A long line still formed to leave the dining area as each boy was searched to make sure he wasn't sneaking out food.

Consuelo tapped him on the shoulder, then handed him a wrinkled piece of paper and a pen. But he couldn't write. Not even his name. Not yet, at least. But he'd change that very soon, now that he had a motive. For today, he'd make do. He drew an animal's head that would have been mistaken for a cow or lizard if he hadn't added a flowing mane and a single horn between its ears. Good enough.

"Hurry up, kid," a guard called to him from the door. Consuelo pocketed the scrap paper as Santiago gathered the sodden napkins from the floor and threw them away before rushing toward the door. For the first time since arriving at the center, he smiled.

The center provided school for them on Mondays and Thursdays. Each boy was supposed to attend two hours a day either in the morning or afternoon, but depending on the guard on duty, sometimes as many as half the boys stayed watching *tele* instead. Lessons took place in another small room off the main one. Long, white plastic tables with four or five folding chairs along one side worked as desks. A whiteboard stood on an easel at the front next to a small, square card table the teacher used. No pens were allowed—nothing that encouraged drawing on bodies. Even the dry-erase marker dangled from a cord around the teacher's neck—black, because blue and red were historically associated with gang colors.

Their teacher, Señor Dante, came from Honduras. Young, tall, and slender with round glasses, turned-up skinny jeans, and a loose tie, he pranced around the classroom unable to stand still for a second. He taught Spanish, English, math, and a little bit of everything else.

Math was the easiest for Santiago, especially since Señor Dante taught it in terms of money. ("If you have twenty-one pesos, and the candy costs one peso and fifty centavos, how many can you buy?" Before the teacher finished asking, Santiago had answered, *"Catorce."* Easy.) But reading and writing, in any language, he'd never learned.

Except now he had to. For Alegría.

From his desk Señor Dante picked up a stack of magazines and began passing them out. "Find an article that gets your attention, read through it, and then tell us what it's about."

Santiago grabbed a magazine with a sigh. This would be harder than he thought.

"Con permiso," said Pinocchio. "I can't read English. Can I get a Spanish magazine?"

"Nope." Señor Dante grinned while he rocked back and forth on his heels. "Try to figure it out. See what words you recognize, and use the pictures to understand what's happening. You have five minutes."

Santiago now thumbed through the magazine eagerly.

Making up stories based on the pictures? That's how he always read!

"This is stupid." Pinocchio ripped his magazine in half. "You can't learn to read if you don't even know the language."

"I understand your frustration," Señor Dante said. "English is a hard language to read. I'm here to work with you, but please don't take it out on my magazine. If the pictures don't help, notice the letters that form the word and the other words around it."

While Señor Dante worked with Pinocchio and the other boys who found the assignment too hard, Santiago made up a story from a picture about two boys close to his age holding a plaque and a comic book. According to Santiago's imagination, the boys had won an award for the comic book they'd written together. The boy with the dark hair looked Central American. Judging by the two colored pencils sticking out from behind his ear, Santiago labeled him the artist and the blond boy with the lead pencil the writer.

"Fantastic! That's exactly what the article says. These boys live here in southern Nuevo México, and their school granted them an award for the comic book they wrote together. *Muy bien*."

"That's cheating," whined Pinocchio, making Santiago glad he no longer sat with him at mealtimes. "That article is in both English and Spanish."

"Not at all cheating," Señor Dante corrected. "Our friend here used the clues accessible to him to figure out what it said. That's exactly what I asked."

Santiago beamed. The words had just been smudges on the page; all the clues had come from the picture. He couldn't even figure out which section was written in English and which in Spanish. He picked out a few words that looked similar in both languages, but had no idea what the words might mean.

When Herrera, the pimply guard who had kicked him the first morning, opened the classroom door to release them back into the main room, Santiago couldn't believe they'd spent two hours in there. Even though it broke a million rules, he stayed behind as his classmates shuffled out.

"I need to write my sister letters, but I don't know how. Can you teach me?" Santiago pleaded.

Señor Dante didn't look surprised at his revelation. Instead, he beamed. "Definitely, that's my job. Just wanting to learn is the most important part."

"García!" Herrera yelled, making Santiago jump. He had no idea the guard knew him from *fulano*.

Had it been Castillo, the nice, bald guard, Santiago would have corrected him—he'd prefer to be called Reyes instead, Mami's last name. But as it was grumpy-pants Herrera, better to not get on his bad side.

"Take this book today, and we'll talk more next time." Señor Dante quickly handed over a large book with a hard cover. It looked beautiful, with drawings of birds and animals on the front. Santiago sighed and tried to hand it back.

"I can't. It might get lost or stolen."

"Then that person obviously needs it more than you."

The guard waved his hands to make him hurry up, but Santiago ignored him. He opened the book as he walked. Each page had an animal, bird, or insect and then a large word followed by smaller words all clumped together. He could copy some of these for Alegría. He remembered what Señor Dante had said about using the images to figure out the words. Along with the picture of a horse, he found a word he recognized. His Tío Ysidro always went to the tavern called El Caballo Entero. Now he'd know whenever he saw this word, *caballo*, that it meant horse.

He sat against a corner in the cold main room to look through the book more carefully, focusing on the large words. He started to notice similarities in the words and patterns, just as Señor Dante had said. For instance, *serpiente* started with the same sound as Santiago. He didn't know how to write his name yet, but the two words probably started with the same letter. He'd have to run this theory by Señor Dante.

After lunch, when the second school group got called, Santiago joined the line, holding the animal book to his chest. Patterson held the door open and didn't bother checking to see who had afternoon school.

Señor Dante smiled at the sight of Santiago but didn't make any comment about his repeated presence. The teacher just made sure Santiago received a different periodical for the story deciphering.

CHAPTER 25

At the end of dinner that night, Consuelo came out with a rag to clean the stand that held the empty trays. Santiago quickly stuffed the mini muffin they'd gotten for dessert into his mouth and walked over with his empty tray.

"I asked a ten-year-old girl to point out your sister," Consuelo mumbled. "Though I should have guessed. She's got your *ojos*."

What? Really? He brought his hand to his eyes. Long lashes tickled his fingertips. Was their shape similar too? He turned to the long serving table, but the stainless steel only distorted his features.

"Did she—" Wait, swallow muffin first. Two gulps later, he tried again. "Is she okay?"

"She asked about you." She reached out for his empty

tray and simultaneously slipped him a piece of paper.

He quickly placed the paper between the pages of the animal book he still had from Señor Dante. He wanted to know the whole story, how Consuelo had managed the inquiry, even the name of the ten-year-old girl who knew Alegría. But the guards called two minutes, and a mob of teenagers brought their trays over to Consuelo.

"You're the best. *Gracias*," Santiago said. Two other guys echoed their thanks when she took their trays. A final nod, and he joined the line to leave, clutching the book tightly to his chest.

The note couldn't really be from Alegría. Not so quickly, when he'd only made the drawing this morning. Maybe Consuelo was sparing his feelings, and the note really came from her.

While the other boys crowded into the TV room off the main room—where, depending on the guard in charge, they watched telenovelas and sports, nature shows and documentaries, or cartoons, all in English—Santiago returned to the corner he had claimed as his own. Under the pretense of reading his book, he opened the folded piece of paper. Three figures with lines coming out of them were drawn in the center, with a large scribble to one side. As Santiago stared at it, he wiped his eyes with the sleeve of his sweatshirt.

Any doubt that the drawing had come from someone

else disappeared. As he looked at it closely, the blobs took shape to form three people. Not just any people, two side by side and the third almost on top of one of the others. Alegría had drawn her family, complete with him carrying her. And the large scribble next to them must be Princesa.

He tucked the drawing back into the book and folded his arms over his knees to give in to the tears. How could someone be so close, but still so far away?

Consuelo had the next two days off. At least Santiago hoped that was the case when he didn't see her. By the third day, he worried he'd gotten her fired. How could he have done that to her? She'd been good and hardworking; she didn't deserve to lose her job. He had no idea smuggling drawings from one group to the other would be a fireable offense. He hated himself for that.

But connecting with Alegría only to lose touch again bothered him more—and then he felt guiltier.

Consuelo finally appeared again at the end of dinner, three days after he'd last seen her. She met Santiago's eyes for the briefest second before shaking her head slightly. Was that an *I can't talk to you; I'll get fired* or *Your sister hasn't given me anything new* headshake?

He clutched the note he'd written during today's class, copying the words Señor Dante had written out for him. His hand had grown stiff from practicing the same words over and over again until the letters finally resembled the teacher's instead of ugly scribbles.

Consuelo suddenly dropped a tray. Runny beans raced under the table. Santiago grabbed a handful of napkins and ducked underneath, hoping the guards couldn't see him.

"She's gone," Consuelo whispered, grabbing the rag and cleaning solution from her apron.

Santiago's head banged against the underside of the table. "What do you mean gone? ¿Está . . . se—" But he couldn't finish the words.

Consuelo placed a hand on his head, soothing the bump. "I don't know. But she's not here anymore."

He crawled out from under the table. His right hand opened and closed to ease the stiffness. Gone. Alegría. Gone. María Dolores. Gone. Mami. Everyone he'd ever loved, gone.

The note he'd meticulously written floated on the remaining bean mess. The pencil marks seemed to glow for a few seconds before sinking into the brown depths.

Alegría, te quiero. Tu hermano, Santiago.

CHAPTER 26

The other boys weren't farting or barking, but
Santiago didn't sleep that night. Every rustle from the
metallic blankets, every muffled whisper, every tick from
the clock, jerked him back to reality.

No, he wouldn't accept this. Not until he knew for sure.
There had to be some mistake. Maybe in the little-girl section everyone wasn't required to go to the cafeteria during
mealtimes. Maybe they were allowed to stay watching television, or the teacher was teaching Alegría how to write
new words. Maybe that's why Consuelo hadn't seen her.

Or maybe Alegría had gotten sick. No, he didn't want
to think about that, either.

Sometime in the middle of the night he got up to
use the bathroom. Five minutes less he didn't have to

try to sleep. A guard didn't follow him in, because one was already there, leaning his back against the tile while Chismoso, the resident gossip, washed his hands. Santiago went about his business and returned to his sleepless spot.

Chismoso.

Guanaco had said Chismoso knew things. Guanaco had also implied the gossiper wasn't trustworthy. Santiago believed Guanaco, but he had to know the truth. The more he thought about it the less he slept.

At breakfast too many people surrounded Chismoso for Santiago to approach him. Instead, Santiago called out across the yard later during their recess. "Hey, Chismoso, can I ask you something?"

"Sure, Santi." The boy grinned, but his brown eyes never stayed still, shifting to take in the happenings within the fenced area. Santiago noticed he never looked him in the eye. Santiago also regretted introducing himself that first day as Santi. Alegría had been the only one to call him that. Coming from Chismoso's mouth, the nickname sounded condescending and malevolent.

"Please, call me Santiago instead."

"Okay, Santi."

Santiago closed his eyes for a second and took a deep breath. "My sister, Alegría García Piedra. She's five and was on the girls' side. Can you find out what happened to her?"

"I might be able to dig something up." Chismoso

looked into Santiago's eyes for the shortest second before returning to his shifting glances around the yard. "For you, Santi. But what are you going to do for me?"

Santiago gulped. He hadn't forgotten that something in return would be expected. He just hadn't wanted to think about it.

Chismoso laughed as if he could read Santiago's thoughts. "Listening's free, but answers are going to cost you."

A muscle in Santiago's jaw clenched.

"What do you want? I don't have anything." Santiago pulled his metallic blanket and toothbrush from his pocket to prove his lack of possessions. The twenty dollars he'd gotten from Don José would be good right now, except he couldn't remember where he'd lost it.

Dread and resolution filled him. Whatever horrible thing Chismoso wanted, Santiago would probably still do it.

"Give me food," Chismoso demanded. "Each meal, every day. Whatever you can sneak out. If you can do that for a few days, I can get you an answer in a few days."

Deadpan now became Santiago's expression of choice. At the end of every meal each boy exited the cafeteria with his pockets inside out to show that he had no food. Rumor was that immortal, plague-ridden mice lived in the facility, and therefore it was strictly forbidden to take any food out of the cafeteria. He'd seen guys frisked while leaving, their secret stash removed, and given a warning that thievery would be added to their records. No one wanted to be moved to an actual criminal detention center.

Chismoso continued. "Three meals a day for four days, that's—"

"Twelve snacks, yes, I know." Santiago crossed his arms over his chest.

Again Chismoso made eye contact for the briefest second before looking away. "Ah, a smart man. I like that."

Santiago kept his glare on the boy. "Does that mean you'll find out about my sister?"

Chismoso smiled wider. "Exactly, after the twelfth, I'll tell you what I unearthed."

Santiago pretended to think about it and then forced a sigh. "Fine."

La malvada had only given him food no one else wanted, when she gave him anything to eat at all. If he hadn't pinched food from her kitchen (or scrounged around the streets), he would have died years ago. Out of all the tasks Chismoso could have given Santiago, sneaking food was one of the few things he felt confident about.

Dinner that night was arroz con pollo with fruit cups for dessert. Normally his favorite meal, because it was hard to mess up, Santiago now agreed with María Dolores. The rice resembled oatmeal in consistency, while the pieces of chicken must have come from the oldest, toughest rooster. To top it off, it tasted of nothing.

Santiago sat at a long table with other guys who ignored him. Asking for Consuelo's help was out of the question—he couldn't risk getting her fired. He ate every last grain and placed someone else's empty fruit cup on his tray. Under his sweatshirt, but over the long sleeved shirt, he tucked his fruit cup into his armpit. Anyone watching would think he was just scratching. He picked up a couple of other trays and stacked them before joining the line. On the side that held the fruit cup in place, he held his metallic blanket, toothbrush, and a new book from Señor Dante in hand. His other hand held up the hems of his shirts to prove he wasn't sneaking any food out.

The guard holding the door was Castillo, one of the nicer ones. Although he wouldn't hold a conversation with the detainees, he didn't ignore them like Patterson did. Or call them crybabies, dirtbags, idiots, or lazy bums like the young, pimply Herrera.

Castillo barely looked Santiago's way as he clicked his counter and Santiago passed him. Once clear, Santiago lowered his shirts and passed the metallic blanket and toothbrush to the other hand to stuff them back into his pockets. The fruit cup remained wedged in his armpit, squeezed just tight enough to keep it secure but not so much it'd explode.

Santiago and Chismoso had decided to make the deliveries in the bathroom stalls. Yes, a guard still kept watch, but Santiago pointed out he wouldn't be able to see anything being passed under the stall dividers. Plus, after-meal bathroom time being a popular event, with or without the iffy Sunday sausages, there'd be nothing suspicious about their regular visits.

Santiago didn't have to wait too long in the corner stall when the person next to him let out a glorious fart.

"Ay, qué rico." Chismoso sighed in relief. A second later the stench reached Santiago. No wonder the other guy had been desperate to let it rip. Santiago waved his hand over his nose before retrieving the fruit cup from its hiding place and holding it under the stall wall. Job done and not needing to be exposed to any more bathroom sensory events, Santiago flushed and exited the stalls.

The next morning Castillo was back on duty during breakfast. This time Santiago hid a fairly straight banana up his sleeve, and Castillo didn't notice the bulge.

Banana delivered, Santiago lined up for the showers, which were too busy to use before breakfast. Chismoso gave him a sideways look coming out of the stalls and spoke to the bathroom at large. An act he often did.

"Herrera's on duty next. He's such a pain in the you know what."

A few of the others groaned, but Santiago knew the

message had been for him—it'd been one thing to sneak food past Castillo, but such trickery wouldn't be possible with Herrera on watch.

Santiago proved him wrong.

At lunchtime, a newcomer two people in front of Santiago was eating his apple as he tried to pass Herrera. Instead of sending him to the back of the line to finish the apple like Castillo would have done, Herrera yanked it from his hand before chucking it at his head.

"Food must never leave this room, ¡*imbécil*!" Herrera screamed. "Do you want mice crawling all over your body? Or are you so used to living that way, you don't care?"

The boy stared at Herrera with wide, frightened eyes. Santiago wanted to reach out, tell him about the food rule, show him the ropes like Guanaco had for him, but he kept his head low, not drawing attention to himself. Not today.

"Oh God, are you crying?" Herrera made a show of being disgusted and shoved the apple boy aside. "Get lost, crybaby, and don't you dare try to sneak food past me again."

Herrera took his anger out on the rest of them by roughly frisking the guy in front of Santiago. Stepping forward, Santiago held his metallic blanket, toothbrush, and book high, and let Herrera pat him down. Once clear, he shoved the ham sandwich that had been wrapped in the blanket into his pocket. Considering that the ham looked moldy, settling for just an apple and a glass of milk hadn't bothered Santiago much.

After dinner, Herrera searched them all again. This time it wasn't until Santiago got to the bathroom that he extracted a small packet holding two cookies from inside his mouth. He handed over the goods and walked out of the bathroom even though Chismoso wanted to talk. With no place to hide, no place to really be alone, Chismoso found Santiago trying to read, leaning against his corner.

"How are you doing it?" he asked, looking down at Santiago.

"How do you find out everything?" Santiago retorted.

Chismoso smiled and held out his empty hands. "A magician never reveals his secrets."

Santiago raised his eyebrows and returned to the book.

The other boy sighed. "Okay, point taken."

"Eight more and you tell me about my sister," Santiago reminded him. "By the way, you have some cookie crumbs on the corner of your mouth."

CHAPTER 27

Santiago snuck food out of the cafeteria after every meal for the next few days, challenging himself to come up with a new way each time. On the twelfth and final meal, he grabbed two small packets of gummy fruit snacks and slipped them into his socks and under the high arch of each foot. One would be for Chismoso, and the other for himself. To celebrate.

As he'd done eleven other times, he held the gummies under the bathroom stall. This time, though, he retracted his hand before Chismoso could grab his loot.

"Tell me first," Santiago insisted through the bathroom stall.

Chismoso responded by flushing the toilet and banging the stall door open. Santiago followed right behind him. The bathroom monitor looked up from his post, but with Santiago ignoring the other boy, their simultaneous exits seemed coincidental.

They stopped against a wall of the main room, careful not to let anyone overhear their conversation. Chismoso turned to Santiago with his genuine smile but shifty eyes.

"I've enjoyed our business so much, I think I'd like a few more snacks before I tell you what I know."

"No."

"But you see, they're serving chocolate cake tonight, and I could use a midnight—"

"Dije que no." Santiago stood his ground. The worst Chismoso could do to him would be to withhold the information, which he was already doing. In the last few days, Santiago had been watching Chismoso. Although he couldn't figure out how Chismoso knew everything, Santiago had learned that the gossiper would nearly combust if he couldn't spill. The truth would come out sooner or later.

"I delivered, and seeing as you're a businessman"—okay, a little flattery couldn't hurt, and Santiago really didn't want to wait—"I expect you to do the same and keep your word. Or maybe the guards will find you tonight with cake covering your blanket." And maybe a little threat couldn't hurt either.

Chismoso brushed imaginary cake crumbs from his

sweatshirt as his eyes narrowed. Santiago waited.

Finally Chismoso sighed and returned to his usual grin, though this time it was definitely forced. "She's not here."

Sneaking out twelve snacks for that? "I know she's not here. But what happened?"

"She got released to her family a week ago."

Santiago reached out for the wall's support. "You're lying."

The forced smile on Chismoso's face changed to his "genuine" one. "Oh no, my friend. I'm not."

Santiago shook his head. "What's the proof? How do I know you're not just making this up?"

"The release papers were signed by María Dolores Piedra Reyes."

The wall no longer held Santiago up as he slid to the floor. His eyes went out of focus, blurring all the figures until the world went dark. Bit by bit, the darkness cleared, and he found himself surrounded by even more devastated teens than when he'd arrived, now over a hundred, all dressed in gray clothes and trapped within four gray walls.

"For another four days of snacks, I can find out more." Chismoso held out his hand for payment.

Santiago raised his gaze. "Like where she went?"

Chismoso scowled, his shifty eyes looking everywhere but where Santiago sat. Finally, the gossiper sighed.

"Immigration papers with that information get sent off immediately. I can't access them."

Still numb, Santiago pulled out the two packets of fruit gummies and placed them in Chismoso's open palm. "There's nothing else to find out."

He lifted the neck of his sweatshirt just enough so that his head hid inside and pulled the hem over his knees. They'd forgotten about him. After everything, they didn't care about him. They'd chosen to leave him behind.

He emerged from his sweatshirt cave to extract Alegría's drawing from inside the book. He'd never see her again, and he didn't want to be reminded of that. Next time he went to the bathroom, he'd throw the drawing away.

CHAPTER 28

It took more than two weeks before the officials called Santiago in for his intake interview. Or rather, two Sundays of the infamous boxed eggs and iffy sausages had passed. When each day more or less started and ended the same, time was easier to count by Sundays.

Most kids got their interview within a few days. The officials must have forgotten about him.

It didn't surprise him. What did was when Castillo finally called him out after breakfast. "Your interview is scheduled now. Do you need to use the bathroom?"

"No." Santiago wiped his sweaty hands on the back of his pants and straightened his shoulders to follow the guard. First impressions counted for everything. But what kind of impression did he want to make? What impression would offer what? No one told him anything.

He knew everyone who came through the facility got interviewed to determine what the government would do with the individual. Sometimes when Chismoso got bored, he told stories about who had cried while being interviewed, or who had claimed to be the illegitimate child of the president. But what resulted from those tales? Chismoso hadn't said.

Still, Santiago could pretend to be brave.

The room in which Castillo left him felt bright and sterile—blinding white walls and fluorescent lights that could be seen from the moon had there been any windows, which there weren't. The effect resulted in a coldness that had nothing to do with the temperature. On the contrary, the temperature in this room was pleasant compared to the perpetual chill that penetrated their main living area.

Two people sat at a table with files of paperwork and gestured for him to sit on the other side. The Latina spoke while the gringo man took notes.

"We have questions to ask which you need to answer truthfully," she said in a voice that came out both patronizing and emotionless. "Do you understand?"

"Yes."

"First, is Spanish the best language for you to communicate in, or do you require a different language?"

He wanted to joke, ease the tension, say something like

good food was the language he best identified with, so having a pork-and-cheese *tamal* present would make communication easier. But these two didn't seem the joking type.

"Spanish is fine," he said.

"What is your full name?"

"Santiago García Reyes."

"When is your birthday?"

"I don't know. Around Easter."

"What year?"

"I'm twelve now, so whatever year that means."

Maybe because he was a kid, or he really looked clueless, they didn't question either response.

"What country do you come from?"

"México."

"And what is your address in México?"

"I don't know," he admitted.

"What village or town?"

"I don't know if it has a name. We just call it *el campo*."

The man and woman looked at each other, communicating telepathically, maybe thinking he was lying. He didn't know what to tell them. He honestly didn't know. *La malvada* lived in a huddle of buildings that didn't have a bus stop—you just told the driver where to let you off or waved along the side of the road when you wanted the driver to pick you up. Sometimes, if you were lucky, the driver did.

"But it's about thirty minutes outside of Chihuahua," Santiago added.

That response received a slight nod from the woman, as if he'd finally said something right.

"Why did you try to enter Los Estados Unidos illegally?"

He paused for a second to think which response would gain the most sympathy, but he noticed the woman's eyes narrow when he didn't answer immediately. "Mami's *madre* beat me."

They didn't seem to hear what he'd said. Or they chose not to believe it.

"Did you come here alone?" the woman continued.

"No," he sighed.

"Who were the people you came with?"

"My sisters." He hadn't intended to lie. With Alegría gone, he knew he'd never see them again. He might have helped them cross the border, even saved their lives, but at the end of the day, he was just some random kid they'd picked up in México. He'd been stupid to think they'd felt otherwise. At the same time, it still resonated as the most truthful thing he'd said yet. In his heart, they had been his sisters.

"Let me remind you"—the woman leaned forward on the table and spoke slowly and extra patronizingly—"that we are U.S. government officials, and we require a truthful statement on your behalf."

"Yes," Santiago agreed.

The woman crossed her hands over her file. "We know for a fact that a mother and young daughter were traveling with you."

Santiago nodded. "That's right. María Dolores Piedra Reyes, *la madre*, and Alegría García Piedra, *la hija*. My sisters."

The woman narrowed her eyes again, then lifted her eyebrows, the first obvious change of expression from her otherwise deadpan face. "Explain."

An involuntary sigh came out of Santiago. Details were key. Details would make any story believable.

"María Eugenia was born first." He mentioned the name of María Dolores's married sister. "Then came María Dolores. After that, my *mamá* met my *padre* and had me."

So far, so true. After all, his own parents had met after María Dolores had been born; and he never actually said María Eugenia and María Dolores were born to *his mamá*.

"Then Padre . . ." He deliberately didn't use "my," so still not lying. "He fell in love with María Dolores and had Alegría. So, sisters."

The man looked up from his notes and gave a slight nod in agreement that these things sometimes happened. Santiago remembered hearing a gossiping relative once say that stranger things happened in real life than in fiction.

The woman accepted the statement with a blink. "Where are your parents?"

"Padre disappeared. No one knows where he went." His voice grew softer. "And Mami died when I was little."

"So, who raised you?"

A muscle involuntarily jerked at the side of his face. He wouldn't lie here—he didn't know what to say instead— but that didn't mean he would be happy about sharing this part of his life either. "I told you. My *mamá's madre*, the one who hit me."

"Your *abuela*?"

How he hated that word in the context of *la malvada*. Someone like her didn't deserve to be called a grand-mother. "Yes."

"What is her name?"

He could refuse to answer. He never called her anything to her face, except once, and that resulted in the burn marks running down his back. If ever there was a name that didn't suit someone it was hers. "Agracia Reyes de la Luz."

"And your mother's name?"

"Sofinda Reyes de la Luz."

"And your father's?"

"I don't know."

"How do you not know your father's name?"

"Mami never talked about him. He left before I knew him."

A weighted silence fell over the room. Oh no, now he'd done it. He'd said too much. He forced his face to remain blank, but he'd messed up, and the woman noticed.

"You said your father fell in love with your sister, María Dolores. How is it you never knew him?"

"I was living with relatives at that time." He continued not lying. It wasn't his responsibility to correct the woman over whose father it had been, or anything else she misunderstood. "Mami had died, and her *madre* hated me, so she'd send me off to different relatives. I didn't know about Alegría until recently, and that's the truth."

Again the pair exchanged questioning looks. Santiago waited in his chair patiently while they came to a nonverbal conclusion.

"Is there anything else you want to tell us?" the woman asked as if she half expected him to confess to being a mass murderer and drug lord.

Santiago straightened up in the chair and licked his lips. If there was any chance . . . "Where are my sisters? Do they know I'm still here? Are they coming back for me? How can I get in contact with them?"

"I'm sorry, that information is restricted."

"But they're my family!" he screamed. So much for making a favorable impression. "The only family I care about."

The woman's mouth twitched as if she was about to tell

him off for being rude. Instead, she turned her attention to the files in front of her and made a show of straightening them. "We're going to look into all of this information for verification."

"Go ahead." He slumped back on the chair. For the first time since Alegría's departure, Santiago felt relief. With her gone, they couldn't prove or disprove his story. His truth.

The man finished scribbling his notes and passed the notebook across to Santiago. "Please read this information and sign below to confirm that everything it says is accurate."

This time Santiago paled. He shifted on his hard chair and avoided making eye contact.

"I can't. I'm still learning how to read."

CHAPTER 29

Santiago lost count of how many weeks had passed. Had it been seven or eight Sundays of boxed eggs?

Then one day they were given the biggest feast of their lives with turkey, stuffing, gravy, mashed potatoes, green beans, and some weird gelled red thing no one but a few brave souls tried. Santiago loved the tang and asked Consuelo to pile extra of the red on his potatoes when they were allowed to get seconds. According to Chismoso (who'd been at the center the longest and had been present at the feast last year), it was some kind of holiday when locals welcomed immigrants by giving them lots to eat.

Yet as Santiago ate the *"pai" de calabaza* (what kind of a person came up with a dessert made from pumpkin?), he couldn't help but think that maybe they were being fattened up for slaughter.

His gut proved correct when the day after the huge feast, a bus parked outside the facility. A large white bus with no letters or design, large enough to hold half the boys in their area. Three boys from the little-kid section, the first Santiago had seen of the others held at the center, were loaded onto the bus, which let out gray clouds of exhaust as if it were digesting the children it had just eaten. Santiago watched this phenomenon with his fingers laced through the chain-link fence that enclosed the outside area.

"That's my brother!" Manzano, the boy who tried to take an apple out of the dining hall, called out. "Where are they taking him?"

The rest of the boys all dashed toward the fence, except for Chismoso, who stood back, looking self-important. "That's the bus to send people back."

Everyone began to talk at once.

"What? To México?"

"No, al Polo Norte, idiota."

"But I'm not Mexican!"

"You think the girls will come out next?"

Boys pressed against Santiago in attempt to see over his tall head. The wire from the fence dug into his hands, but he didn't push back.

"How often does it come?"

"Sometimes every month, sometimes not for three months," Chismoso said, still standing away from the mob by the fence. "Basically whenever you *gachos* have filled up the facility. Did you know it costs more than seven hundred dollars per person per day to keep us here?"

"*¡Mentira!*"

"And they can't afford to give us beds and real food?"

"My dad earns less than that in a month, and he still provides for the whole family."

Chismoso gave a noncommittal response.

"You've been here the longest. Aren't you afraid you're going to be on the bus, Chismoso?"

"Nope."

"*¡Entren ahora!*" Herrera yelled for them to get inside, cutting their outdoor time short before the legendary girls emerged. It took a few minutes before the guys behind Santiago stopped shoving and allowed him to follow. He could still feel the fence digging into his hands. As horrible as staying here would be, it didn't compare with returning back there.

From a clipboard Herrera called out names. Manzano's name came first, except they used his real name, evident by his moving out of the shoulder-to-shoulder line they had had to form. Then Pinocchio and the man-child with the tattoos who'd arrived the same day as Santiago. Three more got called, then ten.

Santiago hung his head low as he waited to be summoned.

"And García."

So this was it. He would have to face his fate. As soon as he could get his feet to move.

Until one of the other boys called out, "Which one?"

Herrera scowled, clearly wanting to say all of the Garcías should get the heck out of there. Instead, he resigned himself to disappointment and rechecked the list. "Guillermo García."

Santiago breathed. He'd escaped deportation. This time.

CHAPTER 30

Not long after, two men and two women came to talk to the boys. Chismoso, with his uncanny connections, knew ahead of time and tried to get his fellow residents excited.

"Think about it, gorgeous women visiting us," the gossiper boasted. The result was that at least half the guys showered before their arrival.

Santiago supposed they were okay-looking, for old people. Certainly not the supermodels Chismoso had promised. Not that it made any difference to Santiago. He showered every morning, because he could, and because it occupied time.

"Hi, everyone." One of the men addressed them in flawless but curt Spanish. "We are volunteers from the Ley Unido nonprofit organization."

A new boy with pale skin and military-cut blond hair (the only blond currently there) raised his hand and spoke in English. "I no speak Spanish."

The older woman of the two asked him a question in English to which he replied, "Russia."

The same woman turned to the teens watching her and said in Spanish, "Who here understands Spanish?"

Everyone but five others raised their hands, the most non-Spanish speakers Santiago had encountered since his arrival. In true fashion, Chismoso explained those five's life stories with a pointed finger. "He's from Syria, those two are Brazilian, and the other two only speak indigenous languages."

The woman waved aside the other five to join her and the Russian boy where she could talk to them privately, but how and in what language?

The man who had started the introduction continued his address to the Spanish speakers. "We're mostly retired lawyers working as volunteers to make you aware of the options available to you as immigrants and refugees."

"My family doesn't have any money," said Llorón, a new, whiny boy. Most of the boys murmured in agreement.

The speaker nodded. "The services we offer here at the center are completely free. For instance, we can help you get reunited with your family or put in group housing, where you can live more freely outside of the center until your immigration status is decided. We can also advise you on the programs you're most likely to qualify for and help you fill out paperwork."

Santiago shifted uneasily from his spot on the floor. All this for free?

"What do you guys get out of this? How do we know you're not screwing us over?" Llorón now crossed his arms over his chest. Santiago noticed that even Chismoso didn't voice his usual smart-mouth responses.

The other man stepped forward, this one with old-age spots on his face and looking more physically frail than the speaker, but with sharp eyes. "We do this because we've been in your situation. We've been separated from our families; we've risked our lives to leave our homes. We have been you."

Silence filled the room. Whatever these people said, their clothes, their education, their mannerisms spoke differently.

"We'll be here all next week, available to talk with each of you individually," the first man continued.

Santiago slumped forward, hugging his knees inside his sweatshirt. Weeks had passed since his intake interview and nothing had happened. Other kids had come and gone in that time. He'd been forgotten, again, but so what? Sure the facility was lonely, cold, depressing, boring, uncomfortable, and—in his mind—completely pointless, considering all the resources they spent in housing him here instead of letting him take care of himself in the outside world.

Like he'd always done.

But, truthfully, he was fed and clothed with a roof over his head. He got to go to school. With Alegría gone, learning to read and write now offered a way to pass the endless time. He knew what to expect. In here no one hurt him. No one made him feel loved only to abandon him later.

Other than with Consuelo and Señor Dante, he talked to no one, and no one noticed him. Honestly, not the worst life he'd lived.

The volunteer lawyers each carried large briefcases when they returned on Monday. A new pregnant woman joined them; young and looking hugely out of place, she smiled.

"*Con permiso*, I got to pee." And she dashed off without waiting for permission or even acknowledgment.

Santiago watched from his reading and sleeping spot in the corner as two frightened teenage boys burst out of the bathroom at the sight of a woman rushing into their private space. But not even the strictest guard dared tell a pregnant woman where she couldn't pee.

A piece of toilet paper was stuck to her shoe when she exited, making a few of the boys snicker. Santiago marked the page with his finger and walked up to her.

"Hold still," he said while pointing to the toilet paper

behind her. He stepped on the trailing end and brushed it toward the wall with his flip-flop.

"You're my savior." She beamed at him.

He gave her a stiff nod and returned to his spot in the corner.

"Wait." She grabbed his arm, which immediately caused him to cower, a defense mechanism he'd developed long ago at *la malvada*'s house. She let go quickly, maybe remembering the "no touching" rule, and rested her hands on her stomach. He didn't move but avoided eye contact. "Why don't you meet with me, and we can go over your case?"

"There's nothing to go over," he said.

"I disagree. Something can always be done, but you won't know until you try."

He didn't want to say yes, didn't want to agree. But his eyes finally met hers, hopeful and kind, and his mouth relented. "Fine."

The room they entered was accessed from the main living room and might have once been a supply closet, just large enough for a small table and two chairs. It was stuffy from lack of ventilation but as a result, warmer than the regular area. She removed a couple of layers of clothes, and his perpetual goose bumps retreated into his arms.

"I'm Bárbara. I work part-time for Ley Unido, which, as you know, is a nonprofit organization that offers legal council to youths in immigration centers, without actual legal representation."

Santiago blinked. "What does that mean?"

"It means I can give you advice on your options and rights, and help with paperwork while you're here, but I can't be your lawyer if you decide you want one."

What good is that then? he wanted to shout. *I thought you said you wanted to help?* Instead he maintained the impassive expression that months at the center had brought on. "So, what are my options?"

"I need to know more about you and your situation back home. You're *mexicano*, I'm guessing by your accent? Tell me about your family. Why you came to this country. Who you have here. The more information you can give me, the more advice or options I'll have for you."

"I've already told the other guys everything."

"What other guys?"

"The officers or whatever they are. The people who work here."

"Ah, but you see, I don't work here." She smiled and reached out for his hand, which he pulled away before she could grasp it. She straightened up and continued, "Their job is to record everyone who comes in and get them out of here as soon as possible. My job is to offer you options that might let you stay in this country."

He didn't want to think too much about this. But hope

suddenly sprouted inside before he could stop it. Darn hope, exactly what he dreaded.

He breathed deeply and told the story he'd told when he arrived. The carefully worded truth, and the internal truth that included two sisters. He made sure it matched with the first report in case the two ever crossed paths.

"Tell me about your *abuela*," she said.

"I'd rather not."

"How come?"

"She's an evil person who hates me."

"What makes you think she hated you?" Señora Bárbara spoke carefully, so as never to put words in his mouth.

Anger rose in him as he explained. "She always screamed at me or insulted me. And that was only when she couldn't throw anything in my direction or hit me." He crossed his arms tightly around his chest.

Señora Bárbara gave him a pitying look before quickly turning away to dab her eyes. "Sorry, baby hormones."

Still, it took her several more minutes before she continued. "I'm not saying you're doing that, but unfortunately a lot of kids say they're being abused when they're not. They think it evokes sympathy so the judge will grant them refugee status. In fact, I know of several kids who were abused, but there wasn't any evidence. The court didn't believe their mistreatment, and they were returned to their abusive relatives. We're going to need more proof than your word."

Proof? Was that all she wanted? He stood up and placed his current book on the table before taking off his sweatshirt and shirt. The room wasn't as warm as he'd thought. Goose bumps rematerialized up and down his arms and along the sides of his visible ribs. The chill also highlighted the redness of his scars. He turned to show his front and back, too many to have been accidental. "I can tell you how I got each one. Some have faded, but I have more under my pants."

"I'm so sorry," she said as she scribbled in her notebook. "And no, I don't need the details. It makes sense that you'd want to escape that. The good news is that the judge should definitely agree that's not a safe environment for you. And she was your legal guardian?"

He pulled the shirt and then sweatshirt back on and curled the bottom ribbing under to hide his cold hands inside. "I don't know if it was legal, but she's the one who took over when Mami died."

"Were you ever in foster care?"

"No, but she tried to get rid of me all the time. Sending me to live with different relatives."

"How many times did this happen?"

He held out his hand to count off as he went through the list chronologically in his head. "Five times? After that there were no relatives left who would take me."

She nodded as she continued scribbling. "Thank you for sharing all of this. I think you're a great candidate to seek asylum."

He remembered Guanaco, his first friend in the facility, and how it wasn't until he turned eighteen that anything changed. "So I won't get sent back? I can stay here while I seek asylum?"

"I can't say anything for sure." She went through her notes. "Ideally, I'd like to get you into foster care."

He looked at his hands, still wrapped in the hem of his sweatshirt. Something else to get his hopes up, something else to disappoint him. If he stayed here, at least he knew what to expect. Into the darkest corner of his mind he shoved the other reason: If he stayed here, María Dolores would know where to find him.

"Maybe foster care isn't a good idea."

Señora Bárbara reached out and took his hands out of his sweatshirt, not letting them go when he tried to pull away. "No one's going to hurt you. Our foster care families are thoroughly screened, and they will welcome you into their homes. You'll live the life of a normal adolescent."

Instead of that of a detainee—or prisoner, since they were virtually the same in here. He could wear whatever he wanted, assuming he had options. Eat anything that was available. Wake up and go to bed anytime, until ordered otherwise. He could dance in the rain, when it happened in the desert.

"I'll stay there until I'm eighteen?"

"Probably not. Foster care is temporary. Until your sister can take care of you."

"She's not coming." Or else she would have gotten him when she came for Alegría. But would it have changed anything if she had? According to Chismoso, youths were only released to parents or *tíos* who could prove they were related. What proof would María Dolores have? He didn't even know his own birth date.

Señora Bárbara took a few seconds before replying. "Even if it's for a short amount of time, you'd be out of this place."

She rubbed her hand over her baby belly.

Mami had done that too. He didn't know how he knew—he'd been inside her belly—but instinctively he did.

Just as he knew Mami would hate seeing him in here, locked up, and unable to live a free life. For her, he'd do it.

"Por favor," Santiago pleaded. "Tell me everything I need to do to get asylum and foster care and anything else that gets me out of here and not returned to México."

He spent the rest of the morning with Señora Bárbara reading him information she brought and filling out forms. He missed school for the first time, and lunch. When Señora Bárbara pulled two protein bars from her pocket and handed him one (either she hadn't been searched before entering or her pregnancy gave her special food privileges), he shook his head and instead asked how to spell *adoptar* for the foster care papers. Finally, she asked him to write a short autobiography in Spanish for the foster families to read.

"What should I say?"

"Whatever you think people should know about you."

His mind went blank. He couldn't think of anything someone would want to know about him. "Can you write it for me?"

She smiled and shook her head. "It's important that it comes straight from you. Your words, your handwriting."

A breath caught in his throat. He could write. Kind of. Señor Dante had taught him the basics and let him borrow a new book to read on Mondays and Thursdays when they had school. Some words like *hola, gracias*, and, even though it pained him to think about her, *Alegría*, he could write automatically, while others he had to sound out letter by letter to get them on the page. Between the books and practicing often, he could write. And maybe he could write his autobiography by himself.

But thinking up the words still troubled him.

"*Mira.*" Señora Bárbara interrupted his thoughts. "I have to pee again, and I'm not allowed to leave you here alone. Why don't you work on the autobiography for a few days and give it to me by the end of the week?"

"You're coming back?"

"Every day this week." Señora Bárbara stacked the papers she'd collected from him. "In the meantime, I'll start getting these filed."

"How long before anything happens?"

"I'm getting the asylum forms in quickly, but it's still going to take a long time. For foster care, I hope to have you in place in a couple of weeks."

His eyes widened. A couple of weeks? That was nothing. "I'll have the autobiography for you tomorrow."

"Perfect. I want to clarify one thing, though." Her smile faltered a bit, and when she replaced it, it seemed forced. "Leaving the facility doesn't mean you can stay in this country forever. You'll still have a court date, and it will be up to the judge to decide if you are granted asylum. It's possible you might still return to México to live with your *abuela*."

His shoulders dropped, and he swallowed in understanding as he followed her out of the room. That would be the worst-case scenario. He resolved, for Mami, to remain optimistic. No point in thinking or worrying about a different future.

CHAPTER 31

It took the rest of the day to write the autobiography for Señora Bárbara. Santiago attended Señor Dante's afternoon class but kept to a corner while working with a dictionary. The lawyer had said to make the autobiography personal, interesting, and honest. How could anyone know what to write about themselves? What did people find interesting? Señor Dante suggested pretending that "Santiago" was a character in a story and to describe him that way. That helped.

Mi nombre es Santiago, he began.

I am twelve years old. I am an orphan (he had to get help from the teacher in spelling *huérfano) from México. I am learning to read and write in Spanish. I am learning some English, too. I hope to keep getting better. I like reading and telling stories. I can*

take care of niños y bebés. I am responsible. I do not get sick. My
teacher says I am smart. I do not know if that is true.

He double-checked every word in the dictionary to make sure he'd spelled it right and was just adding the last accent mark when Castillo opened the classroom door to let them return to the main room. At the other end, the volunteer lawyers stood by the exit door as they waited for Patterson to buzz them out after a full day of meeting with the other kids.

"Wait!" Santiago called out, dashing toward them.

"Walk!" Patterson yelled in English.

"Tome." He waved the biography at Señora Bárbara. "Is this all right? I didn't want to wait until tomorrow to give it to you."

Señora Bárbara glanced over it before widening the smile that looked so out of place at the center. "Exactly what I wanted. I'll be in touch soon."

Santiago backed away from the door and waved.

For the next few days he put all of his energy into getting out of the center and into foster care. He had asked Señor Dante for a letter that reflected his academic achievements. The teacher gave it to him the next class:

Santiago is one of my star students. He always attends my classes eager to learn. I've never seen a student progress so quickly in my five years of teaching. He is always polite and respectful to everyone. Having Santiago in my class is a reminder of why I became a teacher. He is a true joy to teach.

Santiago liked the letter so much, he wanted to keep it for himself.

He now made sure the guards saw him assisting Consuelo with the cleanup after meals. When the guards asked for volunteers, Santiago jumped at the chance to put up the Christmas decorations. The red, green, and silver paper and foil were more depressing than joyful, but Santiago kept those thoughts to himself. Señora Bárbara hadn't *said* he should be helpful, but it made sense to present himself to everyone in the best light.

A few days after another feast, this one in celebration of *Noche Buena*, Patterson wheeled in a dolly stacked with four heavy boxes of donations. Santiago said in his best English, "I you help."

He lifted the boxes off the dolly, which Patterson wheeled away before the boys got any ideas of playing on it (the prospect had definitely crossed Santiago's mind). He peeled the tape off one of the boxes and gasped.

"Oh no, they're just books," said the whiny Llorón, who had come eagerly at the possibility of belated Christmas presents. When he wasn't keeping everyone awake at night with his crying, he always found something to complain about during the day, the result being that most boys learned to ignore him.

Other boys crowded around to check out the selection from the four boxes. Most of the books were in Spanish, though a few were bilingual, with the odd one in another language. One of the boxes contained fat paperbacks, which, after one of the boys dubbed them *almohadas*, were grabbed by several teens. With a crumpled gray sweatshirt over it, the book would become the closest thing to a pillow anyone had.

From the box in front of him, Santiago pulled out activity books with puzzles and games, Harry Potters (or Arry Potta, as the boys called him), and illustrated Bibles. The stack of Donald Duck comics was grabbed out of his hands instantly, a reminder of home, where they were sold at every other newsstand. Even Santiago, who hadn't known how to read, had enjoyed looking through the comics whenever he came across one. He didn't reserve one for himself this time. Under the comics, the picture books started. A familiar blue-and-gold cover winked at him.

"*Ay*," he gasped, and slowly pulled the book out of the box. He gripped it tightly and brought it close to his chest. He moved away from the boxes to his favorite reading corner.

"Look at Santi," called out Llorón. "He's reading a girl's book."

Two or three turned their heads to look but then shrugged indifference as they continued to go through the boxes. Santiago could feel Patterson's eyes on him. *Be nice.* For foster care, he had to be nice.

"Would you like me to read the story to you?" he asked Llorón, gesturing to the free spot next to him.

"I'm not a baby, and I'm not a girl." Llorón walked away with a huff. Relief escaped Santiago. The first time he read this book he wanted to enjoy it alone.

The princess on the cover wasn't one of those who needed rescuing, but wore the suit of a leader and defender. Santiago held the book for several minutes, turning it around in his hands, feeling the smooth, new-looking cover. It smelled of paper, ink, and glue, not of anyone or anything else, as if waiting to make its own new memories with him. His fingers traced over the title illustrated to look like puffs of air: *La princesa y el viento.*

A story about a princess standing up to the wind spirit to protect her people, the one he'd told Alegría in the holding room of this center. The same story his *mami* used to read to him. At the time, Santiago had thought the princess had been Mami. After all, Mami had been able to talk to the wind as well.

He pressed the book against his chest. Even with the

hard cover and pointed edges, it felt soft and comforting. Like Mami. More than ever, he missed her.

He had to get into foster care. It was the only way out. The only way to dance in the rain. A couple of weeks, Señora Bárbara had promised. Just two or three weeks.

He opened the book carefully to not hurt the spine and turned to the first page. As he read it, he didn't need to sound out any of the words. This story he knew.

CHAPTER 32

"*¡Basta!* Get off of me!"

Santiago sat up so quickly his head spun and his eyes struggled to focus in the semi-light. He was back at *la malvada's* house. Hands shaking, he reached for the wall behind him to steady himself.

Where would the blow come from? He couldn't see her. Because she wasn't here. Only teenage boys. And guards.

"Mamá! Mamá, come back!" The screaming continued.

All the boys were now awake, muttering and cursing the screamer. Santiago's heart still pounded, even though it hadn't been he who screamed. He clung to his book like a safety blanket.

Herrera stomped toward a figure thrashing on the

floor as if he were having a seizure. All around the boy, the metallic blanket lay in shreds.

"Wake up, you *loco*." The guard kicked him. The thrashing boy leaped to his feet.

Herrera jumped back and let out a high-pitched squeal. The screaming boy stood there staring at the guard. Slowly the boy turned in a tight circle to glare at the crowded room.

Santiago gasped. It was Llorón, the boy who'd made fun of his book. His wide black eyes looked possessed. And at the same time empty.

"He's still asleep," someone whispered. The room looked on in silence.

"Do something," Herrera told his colleague, a new guard Santiago didn't know.

"Like what? You're not supposed to wake up a sleep-walker. Something about the shock could damage their brain."

Llorón started walking around the crowded room, shuffling his feet like a zombie, though looking more like a ghost. None of the teenagers dared utter a word.

"Maybe we can ease him back to the floor," Herrera said with false bravado.

The other guard screeched. "Are you crazy? You can't touch him. You want to get sued for misconduct?"

"*Llama al médico,*" Herrera ordered.

"No one's on duty. Budget cuts."

Llorón continued weaving around the bodies, causing the boys to squirm out of the way. He came within a meter of Santiago, staring at him with empty eyes.

Santiago set his book down and rose slowly to his feet, not wanting to look Llorón in the eye. He extended his arm and pointed to the floor.

"*Acuéstate*, right now," Santiago ordered in the tone he used when his cousins got out of hand.

Llorón seemed to understand. "*¿Y Mamá?*"

"She's coming," Santiago lied, keeping his voice firm.

"They killed Papi. Trying to cross. They shot him."

"I know," Santiago said, even though he didn't.

"They tried to shoot us, too. Mamá and me. Then they took Mamá away."

"Yes, but you're safe now so lie down," Santiago insisted.

"Here?"

"*Sí, ahora.*"

Llorón circled the floor like a dog before settling down on his side with his arms under his head and his sightless eyes still open. *I should have told him to sleep somewhere else.*

"Now close your eyes," Santiago said. "Keep them closed and Mamá will come."

Finally he shut his eyes, and Santiago exhaled, crumbling back to his corner. A few seconds later Llorón let out a part snort, part moan—a sound that any other night would have had the boys laughing and trying to mimic it.

Santiago motioned to the guards, pointed to his metallic blanket, and then to the snoring Llorón. Understanding, Herrera hurried to get the sleepwalker a new sheet, while the other guard blinked at Santiago and gave him the smallest smile, the closest any guard came to thanking an inhabitant. Good enough.

Santiago pulled his own blanket over his head. While drowning out the perpetual light, it did nothing to shield the snores. But snores were better than screams, reality checks better than nightmares. The next morning when Llorón remembered nothing of the night terrors and teased Santiago again about his girly book, Santiago kept his mouth shut. If that didn't make him the star candidate to get into foster care, he didn't know what did.

The volunteer lawyers finally returned to the center at the end of January. Except Señora Bárbara wasn't among them.

"*Con permiso,*" Santiago asked the elderly lawyer with the age spots on his hands and face. "Is Señora Bárbara coming tomorrow?"

The lawyer tilted his head back to look up at Santiago. "No, *mi'jo.* She's not returning for a long while. She just had herself a beautiful baby boy. Bless them both."

Santiago remembered her pregnancy, of course, but

hadn't realized she wouldn't return once the baby came. He wanted to feel happy for her, but betrayal overpowered him. She had promised she'd be back. She had also said he'd be in foster care in a couple of weeks, six weeks ago.

"Do you know—I mean—what about my applications?" he stammered. "She put me on the list for foster care and other facilities several weeks ago, and I . . . well, I'm still here."

"Don't worry, *mi'jo*. The interns at the office have taken care of everyone's paperwork." The old man pushed up his glasses and gave him a pitying look. "*Pero desgraciadamente*, these things can take several months—for some people, years. The government wants solutions *ahora*, but then takes forever in pushing forth action."

"What about writing letters? To try to convince them." This couldn't be it, not after everything. "I'm a good kid. Always helping. Ask the guards how good I am."

"Every individual's situation is different." The man shook his head. "There are over thirteen thousand youths in facilities all over the country, and this is one of the better centers. Many are living in tents, with metal fences like cages. *Lo siento*, but it's out of our control."

Weeks ago he had thought staying at the center wouldn't be so bad. But the idea of foster care had changed everything. He knew he shouldn't have gotten his hopes up; he shouldn't have planned for the future. He'd made the same mistake with María Dolores.

"Please tell Señora Bárbara I congratulate her on her new baby." The sharp edges of his favorite book, tucked into his waistband for safekeeping, dug into his chest and groin. He shuffled toward the door and started the line to go outside. It gave him something to do.

An asthmatic boy who'd barely been at the center for two weeks skipped around in a circle like a little kid. "Hey, guess what? I've been approved to go into foster care tomorrow. Can you believe it?"

Santiago turned away and pulled the back of his sweatshirt over his head like a hood. Sick kids always seemed to get the favoritism. A part of him wished the boy's foster family would be despicable.

CHAPTER 33

Santiago stood with his back to his *compañeros*, fingers laced through the chain-link fence surrounding their outdoor area. They hadn't been out in days due to the cold and, even now, were only outside so the main room could be cleaned.

The February wind howled, and the clouds above crackled with thunder. A second later icy rain pelted down on them. He heard the scramble of fifty-some teens rush to the door and hug the wall of the building while Castillo fumbled with his key card.

Still, Santiago didn't move. The hammering rain had no effect. Santiago saw no point in shielding himself, no point in dancing, either. No point in anything.

"Hurry up, I'm freezing," Llorón whined to Castillo.

By the time Castillo got the door open and every-one piled inside, Santiago was drenched to the core, his hair plastered to his face. Castillo called and waved him to hurry up. At the door Santiago turned to look at the rain one last time. The first rain he'd seen or felt since that night in the abandoned shack back in México, when he'd refused to return to *la malvada*'s house. The drops changed from clear to white, pelting to weightless. Snow, he realized, before Castillo almost shut the door in his face.

"Can we go back outside later?"

Castillo laughed before speaking. "Are you kidding? Without coats or shoes? You're lucky you actually got to see snow for a second. The other guys will be jealous."

Santiago's wet flip-flops squeaked as he followed the hall back to their main area. His feet squished in the drenched socks. He removed his book from his waistband and held it away from his wet body. In the bathroom he used a towel to dry the hard, wet cover. The glossy sheen had protected most of the book, but the corners of the cover were no longer rigid and had swelled to double their original size. Inside, the edges of the pages warped in small waves.

Once convinced the book had suffered only minimal damage, Santiago busied himself with removing his clothes, wringing them out, and drying his body as best he could before pulling the wet clothes back on. It was Friday, and they wouldn't receive fresh, dry clothes again until Sunday.

Being the middle of the afternoon, the hot water wasn't turned on in the showers.

The perpetual cold air in the main room felt like a punch in the gut when he emerged from the bathroom. He shuffled to his spot against the wall, his legs just barely able to hold his weight.

His teeth chattered as he draped his metallic blanket over himself, hugging it close. If anything, his body shivered more as he huddled in his corner. His book lay on the floor next to him, but for the first time, he didn't feel like reading. Instead, he rested a shaking hand on the cover, just glad to have its presence nearby.

He didn't move until dinnertime. Still damp and violently shivering, he dragged himself to the food line, before a guard forced him. Lunch had been sandwiches with some kind of bad-smelling meat. Because most people hadn't eaten the sandwiches (Santiago had; he ate everything), there were plenty left over for dinner, and they didn't receive their hot meal of the day. He didn't eat a sandwich this time. Instead, he grabbed two cups of fruit cocktail and only got through one; the other he left behind on the table for someone else. If Consuelo was working, he didn't stick around to help her.

Back in the main room, he settled in his corner for the night, covering his head with the metallic blanket that no longer seemed to work its magic of keeping him warm.

His body shook so much, an incessant rattle came from the sheet.

At some point the overhead lights dimmed, marking bedtime. But that's when the screaming started.

"*¡Mamá! ¡Quiero a mi mamá!*" someone kept screaming. Santiago recognized the screams. They came from someone he knew. He'd better shut up before *la malvada* came and made him stop. But he didn't stop. Like someone being tortured.

If only Mami were here. His *mami*, not someone else's. His *mami* who would warm him up and stop the screaming. He wanted his *mami*. Where was Mami? Where was anyone when he needed them?

He thrashed from one side to the other, unable to get comfortable, still unable to get warm. His body broke into a sweat while simultaneously shivering. His damp clothes clung to his body, or was it the sweat that soaked them through?

The lights came back on. To stop the screamer? No, the screamer had stopped, but several people talked. Muttering things he couldn't understand. Why didn't they shut up? It was supposed to be quiet time. Dim the lights again. Make them stop.

But someone was kicking him. Maybe even saying something? He opened an eye to find a uniformed person looming over him.

"Get up, you lazy bum. Time to eat," the guard said.

Santiago pulled the blanket back over his head and got kicked again. Hard, in the back. He gathered himself up, Mami's book in hand, but his legs gave way from under him, and the lights slowly went out, this time completely.

PART 3

CHAPTER 34

Into the unknown: the future

The bed creaks under Santiago's shivering body. Maybe it's not a bed, but a coffin.

If only this whole death thing would hurry up and happen. Then he'd be back with Mami. Things would be fine, and the screaming would finally stop.

Where is he, anyway? Some kind of transitional realm into the "other" world? Has to be. The light hurts his eyes. His body aches—tired and stiff, but not enough to merit screaming. And his throat, so raw—no strength to scream.

So, who's screaming? Or yelling, rather? Not him. The noise hurts his head. Harsh and scolding. Coming from a man, not a teenager. An older white man with white hair, white mustache, and a white coat. Someone Santiago has seen before.

"Extreme negligence on your part," the voice says in English, though the words would have been very similar in Spanish.

Then: "A human . . . his life."

Wait. Did someone "lose" their life? Someone's dead? Is he the someone? Is it possible to die without knowing it?

A fleece blanket covers his body. Underneath him, something molds around his back and head. A bed and a pillow. Comfort. He's definitely comfortable. So he could be dead.

The voice belongs to the doctor who examined him on arrival, his eyes still red, this time filled with rage. The bodies he's talking to become clear: Herrera, Castillo, Patterson, and other guards he doesn't recognize.

He must still be at the center. His head pounding, limbs arching, body shaking. No purgatory, just inferno.

The doctor continues to yell, now saying something about not being able to do his job if the guards don't do theirs. "Not surprisingly, the family is pressing charges."

Even though the doctor only speaks English, the line about pressing charges is familiar—Santiago heard it the few times he watched a courtroom show on daytime *televisión*. The family of the dead is suing.

A lump presses against his already raw throat. Someone

has definitely died. But not him—no one in his family would sue on his behalf.

The doctor issues further insults before picking up a towel and throwing it at Patterson's face. Grabs a gray sweatshirt and flings it at Herrera. Finally, the doctor waves his hand in dismissal. *Quick, eyes close. See nothing, know nothing.* If the guards know he witnessed the scolding, he'll be truly dead.

His throat burns as he breathes through his mouth. He coughs and then chokes from the pain. Things hurt a lot less when he was dead.

When he is sure the guards have left, he slowly opens his eyes again and forces out words. *"¿Dónde estoy?"*

Instead of answering, the doctor holds out a plastic cup full of some red syrup. It tastes like a melted lollipop coating a bitter insect, but it does soothe his throat.

"Where I?" Santiago tries again, this time in English.

"Infirmary."

"¿Eh?"

"Medical room," the doctor clarifies.

The same machines hum as they did when he received his entry physical, the same sterile atmosphere as before. Except this time a book (his book!) sits on a table, and two cots are positioned against the wall—his, and an empty one.

A tousled blanket remains on the empty cot. Someone had been in it.

Consuelo enters the room bearing a tray laden with food. Santiago turns his head to follow the delicious smell, using every bit of strength to push himself to his elbows and then to sitting.

She places the tray on his lap. "*Sopa de pollo*. I made it especially for you and the other sick . . ." Her voice trails off, and she excuses herself from the room as tears run down her face.

Santiago's hand reaches for her. *Wait, don't leave*. He lets out a hacking cough instead.

"Who boy died?" Santiago asks in English once he's able to talk again. "What he name?"

The doctor returns to his side with another cup, this time holding a long white pill, a round peach-colored one, and a capsule. "Mendez. Lorén Mendez."

The name isn't familiar. Maybe it's one of the little boys. Or someone from his section he only knows by nickname. But the doctor doesn't seem to be in a chatty mood, going through paperwork and scowling. Maybe Santiago is better off not knowing right now.

The soup, cool enough to eat, hot enough to soothe, tastes *a gloria*. Tender pieces of poultry cover the bottom of the bowl along with real carrots and peas.

On the tray, Consuelo included a soft, warm roll with a pat of butter, an orange and a banana, a purple Jell-O cup, and a glass of grapefruit juice. His shrunken stomach cries for him to stop, while the rest of his body yearns for the nourishment. He's never swallowed pills before, but they go down nicely hidden within the Jell-O.

Before finishing the juice, he raises the glass toward the empty cot.

"It should've been me, Lorén. I could've been with my *mami*, and no one would care."

CHAPTER 35

Santiago stays in the infirmary for the weekend, until his cough disappears and his strength returns. Every mealtime, Consuelo brings him a different soup—lentil, beef, tortilla. Each one homemade, each one probably paid for from her own salary. He insists she doesn't need to, and she insists she wants to. In exchange he tears out a page from a magazine the doctor has, writes *muchísimas gracias* on the top, and presents her with a picture of a flower bouquet.

The doctor releases him in time for Señor Dante's Monday afternoon class. Everyone stops their boredom to stare. Some back away like they did with Llorón's sleepwalking. Others gawk like they're witnessing some kind of phenomena. Thanks to Chismoso, everyone knows more about Santiago's medical state than him.

"Is it true you almost died of hypothermia?"

"*Mano*, I saw you faint. That was some scary stuff."

"Where did you stay?"

"Did you see the dead body?"

Too much, too many. Santiago cowers from the mob, covering his head with his arms. "Please, just leave me alone."

He needs somewhere to hide. The bathroom? No, a different open door beckons. He darts into the classroom and slides into a folding chair near the teacher's desk in the front. "Save me."

Señor Dante nods without question. He walks to the door and calls the class in. *"Chicos, vamos."*

Once the afternoon teens enter, the teacher turns to the class and addresses them all in English. "Today, anyone who wants to talk has to do so in English."

"¿Por qué—"

"No, English."

A grumble echoes through the room as Señor Dante throws out questions like "What is your favorite animal?" and allows squawks and roars in lieu of responses when the boys don't know the name in English.

Santiago meets the teacher's eye and mouths, *Gracias.*

Señor Dante raises his eyebrows, waiting. Santiago's lips form new words. *Thank you.*

Señor Dante blinks in acknowledgment and continues teaching.

The nighttime screaming stops with the death of Lorén Mendez, and several things change in the center.

People from the outside visit and inspect the facility: politicians, lawyers, and reporters. Heads shake, interviews are conducted, and more scolding is done, but their standard of living doesn't change much—no beds and food that's only sometimes edible. The exception is their clothing.

Now if their clothes get wet, they're required to ask for a dry set. No exceptions. In a room full of bored, mischievous teenagers, a lot decide to take showers with their clothes on. And the guards can only keep issuing dry clothes.

Also, if they're cold, they have the right to additional clothes. For a few days, a group of boys go around with underwear on their heads as skullcaps until the joke stops being funny. A real thing that becomes popular is to use an extra pair of socks as mittens; Santiago's live in his pockets along with his toothbrush and metallic blanket. His book still lives in his waistband.

Turns out the metallic blankets only work by retaining heat. Señor Dante explains the science of it, and they even conduct an experiment with a lamp and a cup of ice. It would have been a cool class if their lives hadn't depended on it.

But most of all, the guards now actually pay attention to everyone, shifting their eyes from one boy to the next like special agents, except without the sunglasses. Chismoso swears the doctor actually shouted, "Make sure you check on the boys you're paid to protect instead of standing around counting the fleas on your arms."

Anyone who gets sick receives a dose of nasty-tasting medicine. Lesson learned: If you're only a little sick, you use up all your weakened energy to pretend you aren't.

Who knew that even in death Lorén Mendez, the whiny sleepwalker the boys called Llorón, could cause so much trouble?

CHAPTER 36

The spring winds continue to kick up as February wears on, gathering dust and dirt and flinging it into Santiago's face, the only person brave or stupid enough to confront it. Some days the wind blows so hard that the guards cancel the boys' outdoor time. No fresh air, no fantasies of what it's like beyond the chain-link fence. Everything exactly the same, every day no different from the rest.

Only the two days of school change the monotony. Even within the same day, no two sessions are exactly the same, and they're always interesting.

"Today, we're going to work on our writing," Señor Dante says as he passes out paper and pencils.

Santiago sits up and ignores the surrounding moans.

"Why is writing important when there's so much technology out there that can do it for us?" Señor Dante asks.

"Because you can't always depend on technology," says a Guatemalan nicknamed Listo for his tendency to answer the teacher's questions first.

Señor Dante nods. "Exactly. Technology fails all the time. Computers crash; phones run out of battery."

"Not everyone has phones or computers," another boy says.

"Like us." The comment is met with groans.

Señor Dante persists. "Why else?"

"'Cause if you never write to your *abuelita*, she'll never send you money for your birthday."

The class laughs and many agree.

"Very true." The corner of Señor Dante's eyes crinkle in a grin. "My *mami* doesn't know how to turn on a computer and only has a house phone. My *abuelito* in Honduras doesn't have any of those. *¿Qué más?*"

"It's a way to express yourself," Santiago says to himself. Except he says it out loud.

Señor Dante pounces on his words as he points at him eagerly. "Expand."

"I don't know." He thinks about it for a second. "When you write, you put something of yourself onto the paper. A person can tell if you're sad or insecure based on how you've written something."

"Perfect, I love it."

"Also," Listo interrupts. Teacher's pet. "Writing by hand makes it easier to work nonlinearly."

Señor Dante prances from one side of the room to the other, barely able to contain his excitement. "Tell us what that means."

Listo straightens up in his chair.

"Kiss-up," Chismoso mutters.

"Well, like, on a piece of paper, you don't have to write in straight lines." Listo shows off. "You can write something in the middle, then something different at an angle near a corner. You can turn the page upside down and write something that way."

"Wonderful!" Señor Dante claps. "And I want to encourage you to try and think nonlinearly. 'Think outside the box,' *como dicen en inglés*. Not everything has to be methodical. Writing is an art, and through this art you're expressing yourself and not depending on a machine."

"So we can write whatever?" Chismoso raises his eyebrows, checking to see how much he can get away with. *"¿Pero en inglés o en español?"*

"Español." Señor Dante takes a quick inventory of the class. Everyone present speaks Spanish. "The topic is: If you could do anything, what would you do? If you could be anyone, who would you be? Be as realistic or imaginative as you like. If you're attending college, tell me what you're studying. If instead you're sprouting wings and flying

yourself into outer space, I want to know. Write ideas and dreams, or fully thought-out plans. Don't worry about lines, spelling, or presentation. Just write from the heart. And go!"

The blank page in front of Santiago blinds him. His writing has certainly improved. Not perfect, but competent enough. Normally he likes Señor Dante's nonstructured assignments, but thinking about what if? The future? Even an imaginary one would be devastating when it didn't come true.

He thought he could have a better life by coming to the U.S., assumed he'd live with María Dolores and Alegría together as a family. Stupid. Then there were all those forms for foster care, helping the guards, all in hopes of getting out of here. All for nothing.

His future will be fairly simple: stay here until he turns eighteen and then work the streets back in México, begging for food and scrounging through dumpsters for anything he can find. Returning to work for Don José would only remind him of everything he wants to forget.

There's no future for him. He'll do nothing, be no one; no point in writing that down.

His *compañeros* aren't as realistic. A few boys share what they wrote with the class: get a job, get married, build a house. Others present their scribbles of random notes: learn to drive, meet a famous person, drive a sports car with the famous person as a passenger. Pathetic.

He crumples the paper into a tight ball. Except Señor Dante catches him. Disappointment shadows the teacher's face. Maybe he should have written something outlandish just to fill the page: owning a pet unicorn—no, no unicorns. That creature will forever remind him of Alegría and her drawing he shouldn't have thrown away. He can't think of what he's lost any more than he can think of what he can never have.

Castillo opens the classroom door. No lingering today, Santiago has to get out.

"Please stay," Señor Dante says to him.

Santiago glances over at Castillo, who waves him the okay. Herrera would have screamed at Santiago to get his lazy butt out of there. If only the mean guard were on duty this time.

He could leave anyway, but the teacher did say please. His eyes focusing on the table, Santiago sits back down on the folding chair. Señor Dante perches on the table in front of him.

"I saw your empty page. What's going on?"

Santiago shrugs, still staring at the table. "I didn't have anything to write."

"I don't believe that. I've seen how creative you are. C'mon, talk to me," the teacher insists.

Santiago plays with the hem of his sweatshirt, folding his

hands over and under until they disappear. But the words linger in the air. "There's no point thinking about what I want to do when there's nothing to look forward to."

Señor Dante sighs. "I get it. You're locked in a facility even though you've done nothing wrong except want a better life, and you don't know when you're getting out."

Yeah, he gets it. Still not looking at him, Santiago adds, "And no one has any control over what happens in the future."

"Maybe not total control. But you can work for what you want, what you believe in. You can control how you respond to what comes your way."

No, he can't. Because he won't be able to change anything. Just like he won't be able to control what this government finally decides to do with him at eighteen. They'll make the decision, and no action from him will change that.

"Okay, let me ask you a different question." Señor Dante's voice softens, as if he understands Santiago's thoughts. "If you could have any job in the world, what job would that be?"

"I don't know."

The teacher crosses his arms over his chest and waits.

Santiago hugs his knees and rests his head on top of his legs. Any job in the world? He's never thought about it. His family worked whatever jobs brought in money for food, no matter how horrible. Mami did . . . no, he can't remember. Had things worked out with María Dolores, he could have worked in her sister's restaurant, like he did months ago in Capaz. But he wouldn't want to do that for the rest of his life. But what else? What is he good at? What would he want to do instead?

"I guess I wouldn't mind being a teacher. Like you. But for little kids. Four, five, and six are good ages." The words surprise him. Then don't. A part of him already knew.

"Why are those good ages?"

"They're young enough to still believe in unicorns."

Santiago looks up from his knees to catch Señor Dante blinking a few times behind his glasses. "I think you're going to be a great teacher."

Except Señor Dante is the first person in Santiago's life who's encouraged his education. Before coming here, no one cared to show him how to read or write. "Once back in México, no one's going to pay for me to continue going to school."

"So pay for it yourself."

"I don't have any money."

"Then earn it. Do whatever it takes to accomplish your goals," Señor Dante insists.

Yeah, that sounds good in theory, but in practice? *"¿Y si no puedo?"*

"No one succeeds by giving up."

Santiago glances through the open door into the main

room, where kids are lining up for lunch. Castillo forgot about him. Or maybe trusts him. If his stomach weren't starting to growl, he could get away with staying in the classroom with Señor Dante all through lunch.

"Please think about it." Señor Dante holds out his hand.

Santiago accepts the shake. Maybe he *can* be a teacher. He'd be good at it too. And it's something he would enjoy. Better than washing dishes. Better than anything else he can think of. "Okay, I will."

A few weeks later Patterson holds the door open to urge the boys out of the classroom. Señor Dante speaks to the guard quietly in English. Patterson narrows his eyes then agrees. "Five minutes."

The guard leans against the jamb, looking bored, while Señor Dante turns to Santiago. "The government is restricting funding for these centers, saying that education is a luxury they can no longer afford."

"So, you're saying . . ." Santiago speaks slowly, desperate not to let resentment seep into his words. "You won't be our teacher anymore?"

Señor Dante shakes his head, breathing in sharply as if there are many opinions (and bad words) he wants to say, but doesn't. "This is my last week teaching."

So this is it. Santiago turns to leave, but Señor Dante

grabs his arm. The teacher retracts his grip before Patterson notices. Santiago stops, unable to look him in the eye. At least the teacher is saying good-bye.

"The government won't pay for education anymore, but I believe in delivering bad news first," Señor Dante says.

Santiago lifts his head. Does this mean there's good news? How can anything be good after this?

"I'm working with a nonprofit literacy organization." Señor Dante straightens his round glasses and stares at him. "The center granted me permission to start a story time for the younger boys, reading to them for about a half hour twice a week."

Santiago crosses his arms over his chest. Not what he would call good news. Not for him at least. "The little kids are lucky to have you."

"I know you've had many disappointments in your life, but you have to accept the possibility of good things too." Señor Dante perches against a table with his own arms crossed. "Why do you think I've mentioned this to you?"

How should he know? He doesn't care about a reading program for the little kids. He can't join them. Unless . . .

"You want me to read to them? Read them stories?" he gasps.

Patterson shifts from his spot by the door, and Señor Dante quickly holds up two fingers.

"A couple more minutes. Please," the teacher says in English to the guard before returning his attention to Santiago. "I've been approved to have a teen helper, and I think you'd be great for the job."

Him, Santiago. A future teacher. Doing something he's always loved. Except now he would be reading the stories, instead of just telling them.

"*¿En español?*"

"*Claro.*"

Santiago blinks. Excitement—and panic—courses through his body. Señor Dante is serious. He actually wants Santiago to read to the little kids. Santiago will get to go to a different part of the facility. Be someplace new.

"Are the girls getting story time too?" If there's any chance the girl who knew Alegría is still there . . .

Sadness clouds Señor Dante's eyes. "I've only been approved to read to the boys."

Just as well. She is probably long gone. Like everyone else.

"You think I can read well enough?"

Señor Dante turns the question around. "Do *you* think you can read well enough?"

"Maybe?" And because Señor Dante seems to expect a different answer, Santiago corrects himself. "Yes, *creo que sí.*"

CHAPTER 37

Not even two minutes pass after leaving the classroom and joining the lunch line before Listo, the smartypants boy, steps up behind Santiago and nudges him in the back of the legs. "I heard from Chismoso that you're joining Señor D. on a field trip to the little-kid section."

Santiago turns slightly from the single-file line and shrugs, neither confirming nor denying.

"Why do you get to go and not the rest of us?"

"He knows I have experience with kids," Santiago answers as simply as possible.

"You? You never speak to anyone. Most people here don't even know who you are, and you've been here forever."

Santiago keeps his eyes forward and shrugs again.

"I have seven *hermanos*." Listo leans in like a pesky fly to his ear. "I know kids. How many siblings do you have?"

The lunch line starts moving. Listo knocks into his legs again. Santiago stumbles and crashes into the guy in front of him. Gathering his feet under him, Santiago whips around to face Listo.

"Stop. It," Santiago hisses. He narrows his eyes for a second, staring Listo down, then hurries to catch up with the line. The guy in front of him glances over his shoulder as Santiago approaches.

"Sorry, man," Santiago apologizes. "I didn't mean to crash into you."

"'*Tá bien*," the guy mumbles. He's new, probably about sixteen, and already dubbed Sumo for being built like a wrestler.

"You're not getting away with this," Listo insists as he cuts in front of Santiago. "I'm seeing Señor D. after lunch."

"Go ahead," Santiago says. If Listo wants to cut in line, fine. At lunchtime they always get sandwiches in various degrees of staleness or sogginess. Let Listo get a bad sandwich first.

But take the reading program away from him? Not without a fight.

Santiago inhales his sandwich without knowing what's in it and is first to form the exit line. No helping Consuelo today. From the corner of his eye, he sees Listo chug his juice, but not before Sumo joins Santiago in line. Santiago smiles. It's one thing for Listo to cut in front of Santiago—but he won't dare do it to Sumo.

"You don't like sandwiches?" Santiago asks the big guy. "At least today's aren't moldy."

Sumo shakes his head as he shifts uncomfortably on his feet. "I have a severe wheat allergy."

Poor guy. Santiago's own gut handles just about anything, whether it resembles food or not; he never thought about those who can't handle actual food. "That's tough. Did you mention anything when you got brought in?"

Sumo pats his belly. "Yeah, but I think they think I'm faking it."

In other words, the officials who run the facility don't care. As far as they are concerned, providing any food serves their humanitarian requirements.

And there's nothing Santiago can do to change that. But maybe he can give Sumo something to look forward to. Most of the sandwiches are gone, which means they won't be served again for dinner.

"Hey, Chismoso," Santiago calls out. "What's for dinner tonight?"

"Arroz con pollo," Chismoso answers without demanding payment. It must be public information by now. Another reason most of the lunch sandwiches are gone.

"I like arroz con pollo." Sumo smiles.

"Don't get too excited," Santiago warns. "Even I think it's pretty bad. But at least it doesn't have wheat, and there's usually plenty."

"Thanks."

After inspection, Santiago follows Herrera down the hall. Once back in the main area, he dashes to the door of the classroom. The government hasn't dismissed their teacher yet.

"Walk, García!" Herrera shouts.

"Señor Dante," Santiago blurts. "I really, really want to read to the little kids. Please don't take it away from me."

"It's your job." Señor Dante looks up from what might be his final lesson plan. "Why would I—"

Listo appears in the classroom doorway slightly out of breath. "Señor, I'm much more qualified for the reading program. Santi is illiterate."

"Santiago," Señor Dante corrects, "has come a long way. I have never seen that drive for learning."

"But you didn't even give me a chance. *No es justo.*"

Señor Dante steps out from behind his desk and sits on one of the long tables with his arms crossed. "Why do you want to do it?"

"I learned how to read when I was four," Listo brags. "I've won many academic awards in my school, and I've scored higher in tests than people two or three years older than me."

Señor Dante nods and turns to Santiago. Nerves tap-dance on Santiago's stomach. He can't compete with any of that. When he reads, he still has to sound out many words. But Señor Dante said a person needs to do whatever it takes to achieve what they want. And Santiago wants this. He would be good at it too.

Deep breath.

"I grew up hearing stories from my *mamá*." Santiago starts softly and then speaks up as his confidence builds. "Later, I told stories to my cousins, and finally to my . . . my little sister. Stories transport me and listeners to different worlds. For a few minutes, we forget we're stuck in an immigration holding center and remember what it's like to be free and belong somewhere."

A hand claps onto Santiago's shoulder. He yelps as he cowers. Turning, he sees Sumo behind him. No guard tells Sumo off for touching, and his hand feels nice and supportive, now that Santiago knows whose it is. Other boys filter into the classroom, attracted by the crowd.

Santiago smiles his thanks.

"I'm sorry." Señor Dante glances back at Listo. "Santiago is still the right person for the job."

Sumo's cheers and Listo's complaints bring Herrera over to investigate the commotion. Sumo drops his supportive hand from Santiago's shoulder without being told.

Instant silence.

Señor Dante nods. "I'll check with the board about additional teen readers, and, if approved, anyone else can apply. Until then, Santiago will work the reading program."

Listo opens his mouth but then huffs off to the TV room. He probably never even wanted to read to the little kids; he just didn't like not getting something. Herrera leaves the classroom and yells across the main room for the rest of the afternoon pupils.

A boy Santiago has seen around but who hasn't received a nickname yet approaches Señor Dante. "I'd also like to read to the little kids if you're allowed more than one helper. My *hermanito* is there. He was sick when we came. I'd like to make sure he's okay."

The boy's words pierce Santiago's heart. The thought resurfaces of Alegría in the little-girl section, alone. Not knowing what was happening to her or even if she was okay had been torture. After all these months, the memory of feeling powerless to see her still haunts him.

"You should read to the *chiquitínes* for now," Santiago says, stuffing his hands into his full pockets. "I can read to them later."

He has five more years here before they kick him out. What's a few more weeks?

"Santiago," Señor Dante says. "I offered you the job because you'd be best for it."

Santiago stares at the floor. Just because he would be

the best doesn't make it right. "I can't keep him away from his brother."

"Don't do it," Sumo argues. "You wanted this so bad. You fought for this. At least alternate days."

Alternate? The weight of self-sacrifice lifts. Go once a week instead of twice? Air fills his chest once more. A look toward Señor Dante says it's Santiago's choice. He turns to the other boy, who looks hopeful.

"Yes," Santiago says. "Let's share the job."

The other boy's brown eyes widen then quickly narrow. "What do you want in return?"

Santiago exhales and smiles. "Nothing. I got separated from my family too."

CHAPTER 38

Stand straight. Be polite. Try not to attract too much attention.

Holding three books tightly to his chest, Santiago waits while Señor Dante convinces Herrera that Santiago does have permission to leave the big area with him.

"I have a letter from the board of directors saying that I can delegate one of the teen boys to join me for the story time." Señor Dante shows the guard a letter. "I did this with Pablo a couple of days ago; today's Santiago's turn."

"I don't care about the letter. I'm saying we're short staffed. I'm on my own at the moment, and there's no spare guard to escort you two."

"With all due respect, Señor Herrera," Señor Dante says in Spanish with a slight edge to his voice. "What kind of trouble do you think he's going to get into in the hallway? Neither of us can leave through the windowed door without getting buzzed through."

"García's a criminal." Herrera spits on the floor. "You can't expect me to trust him."

The muscles around Santiago's mouth twitch. A criminal? This guard should be locked up for his criminal treatment of them—kicking them and calling them names any chance he gets. Though he can't remember, Santiago's willing to bet Herrera was the one who kicked him in the back when he had hypothermia. But Santiago says nothing. Nothing to upset Herrera more and keep Santiago from reading to the kids.

But Señor Dante is not a "criminal"; even as their former teacher he has power. "Santiago is a refugee, not a criminal. And I'd advise you stop treating him and the others as such. Now, are you going to let us through, or do I need to contact your supervisor?"

Herrera's jaw clenches. Tall and skinny like Santiago, Señor Dante is no match for Herrera, whose pimples don't hide the fact that he's been in fights before. But unlike Santiago, Señor Dante doesn't falter under the threat.

The guard finally relents, scanning the pass around his neck to let them through the door.

"Thank you," Señor Dante says courteously while Herrera scowls.

And as a final blow, Señor Dante places a hand on Santiago's shoulder, fully violating the "no touching" rule, and guides him through the door. Part of Santiago cheers for Señor Dante. The other part wants to warn his *compañeros* to stay clear of Herrera today.

The hallway leads past several closed doors. At one point Santiago sees the windowed door that goes to the intake room, then to the office, and finally to freedom, if he could get through the gates before they shut on him again. So close.

They come across one person in the hallways: a tall, gringa-looking woman in a nice green-and-gold pantsuit that definitely isn't part of a guard's uniform.

"Señora Mariño." The teacher greets the woman in Spanish with the traditional kiss on the cheek. "Still making deliveries?"

"Sadly, yes," she says with a sigh, holding up two baby bottles full of milk. "I'm hoping this is the last day."

"Good luck."

As soon as she disappears into a room, Santiago asks, "What's that about?"

Señor Dante takes his time answering but doesn't hide the bitterness in his voice. "She's an immigration lawyer. Every day for the last week she's been delivering breast milk from her client to her client's baby."

"They took a baby away from her mother?"

"Everyone is separated."

Like him and Alegría. Like Pablo, the boy who wanted to check on his brother.

Señor Dante stops walking and glances around to make sure they're alone in the hallway. "Most of your *compañeros* were traveling alone, trying to escape violent drug gangs, political conflicts, or extreme poverty in their country; a lot have had to rely on no one but themselves."

Gangs? Politics? Yeah, Guanaco, his Salvadoran friend, mentioned something like that. But most of the boys don't talk about their past. Not that he hangs out with them to know. Sometimes, when Chismoso's bored, he fills everyone in on arrival gossip—some boys get caught while trying to cross the border or very close to it; a few, like Santiago, are rescued from the desert; others come from different facilities, where they were housed in massive cages or tents. But a lot of the boys seem to come to the center because they turn themselves in at the border, in hopes of asylum.

The hallway remains empty, and Señor Dante continues in a lower voice. "But most of these younger kids we're going to see were traveling with their parents, adults who shielded them from the horrors you well know. They get here, and suddenly they're alone. They don't know why, and they think they'll never see their family again. No one takes care of them, and they feel like no one cares about them. That's why this reading program is so important. To show we care."

Santiago clenches the books tighter to his chest. It must have been horrible for Alegría. She wouldn't have understood. Just like he hadn't when Mami got taken away. "Why do they separate us?"

"Because they can."

The little-kid area looks the same as the one for the older boys—one main room with doors to one side and access to the bathrooms. Like the older kids, they have no toys.

The main difference is the noise. Two kids scream nonstop. Several huddle against the walls crying hysterically. One boy stops banging his head against the door because they enter. And only some of the ten- or eleven-year-old boys (but no adults) do anything to console them.

"I can't do this." Santiago's voice croaks. It's too much. It's one thing for Santiago to feel this pain—he's used to it; he knows how to live through it. But these boys, some as young as three, away from their parents, being in this prison . . . It's not right. They shouldn't have to endure this.

Señor Dante grabs his hand. "I know—it's heart-rending. But for a half hour, as you said, you can help them forget and give them comfort they haven't felt since their arrival."

Santiago strokes the back of his book, the one Mami

read to him. When Mami died, she left memories. Those memories still offer Santiago comfort all these years later. If anything, these boys need happy memories and comfort. Darn Señor Dante for always being right.

"*Está bien.* I'll stay."

More than fifty boys, ranging from three to eleven years old, notice the arrivals. They rush toward Señor Dante and Santiago in gray blurs.

"Walk!" one guard shouts.

"Stop it!" Another claps his hands in a poor attempt to maintain authority.

A third guard—they have three apparently, though could use several more—grabs one of the running boys by the arm and lifts him off the ground, hissing at him to stop being a pain in the behind. Except he doesn't say "behind." Whatever these guards are trained for, childcare isn't it.

Señor Dante places one finger on his lips, raises the other hand in the air, and makes a V (or bunny ears) with his fingers. He waits patiently, and within five seconds the crowded room falls quiet as the boys sit on the hard floor. Even the two screamers and a couple of the criers cease their outbursts.

"*Buenos días, chicos,*" Señor Dante calls out.

"*Buenos días, Señor Dante,*" they respond, twitching and waiting in their spots.

"The other day we had Pablo, and today my friend Santiago will read to you. He also lives here in the center with you guys." Señor Dante gestures toward him.

Santiago waves while the youngsters gawk at him like he's a movie star. Heat rises up from the back of his neck. How embarrassing.

The kids divide into two groups: Santiago will read picture books to the younger kids in one area of their main room and Señor Dante a novel to the older ones.

Miraculously, they remain quiet, waiting. Santiago takes a deep breath.

He fumbles over the words in the first two pages of *La princesa y el viento* even though he knows the story by heart. The kids still stare at him. All thirty-some. He turns the book around and hides behind the cover while showing the boys the illustrations.

"Is this a girl's book?" a four-year-old asks.

Santiago shakes his head. Maybe Llorón would listen now. "It's a people's book. Everyone can read it."

The boy crawls closer. Santiago reads the next page perfectly. The boy continues to come closer and tries to climb into Santiago's lap. Two others lean against his shoulder to get a better look at the pictures. Immediately, a guard is at their side.

"Get to the back," the guard yells. "No touching."

Santiago bites his lip. What he would give to have

Alegría or his little cousins sitting on his lap during story time. How he misses that.

He rises to his knees and holds the book out so even the castigated boys in the back can see the illustrations and feel the story's invisible embrace. From memory he recites the princess's admonishment to the wind for scattering her villagers: "There's no place you can send us where we won't belong."

He doesn't know the other books by heart but makes sure to stop and point out illustration features for everyone to see. The lap climber somehow wiggles his way back to the front of the group through the course of three books.

"Again, again!" the boys call out when Santiago finishes the last book.

Santiago smiles and hugs the books to his chest. Comfort and escapism. He can do this. "I'll be back—I promise."

CHAPTER 39

Santiago and Pablo continue taking turns reading to the little kids. When Señor Dante gets permission for an extra reader, Listo joins them once before declaring the kids are brats, *malcriados*. Santiago silently thanks which-ever "brat" scared him off.

Unlike the older boys, most of the little kids leave the center within a week. Still, it's way too long. A lot happens in a week. Señor Dante says that being forcefully separated from a parent for a day can traumatize a child for life. Just seeing his buddy, the lap climber, called away during story time, tears Santiago up. Too much like Alegría—even after all these months, he can't forget her.

By his calculations, considering he arrived in the fall when the nights were getting colder and it's almost spring now, he's been at the facility for about six months. No one besides Chismoso has been in the older-boy section as long as him. Many only stay a few weeks; several others board the bus that takes them back to México.

Each time the bus pulls into the parking area, Santiago's throat goes dry. Heat, dehydration, memories. Santiago remembers Chismoso saying it costs over seven hundred dollars per person per day to keep them at the center. Sooner or later the officials will do the math and figure out he isn't worth keeping five more years. Then his name isn't called for the bus and he breathes again, remembers he will be here until he's eighteen, and forgets about deportation until the next time.

The bus doesn't come regularly, never even on a specific day. But instinct says it'll be here soon. What felt like a packed space with ninety-some teens when he arrived now threatens to burst with almost double the amount. So when the bus comes, his gut says he'll be on it. The tightness in his throat agrees.

"Who's on the next bus, Chismoso?" Santiago breaks down and asks. After all these months, the secret to Chismoso's information is still a mystery. Maybe Chismoso bribes (or blackmails) a guard, or provides him with favors in exchange for all the intel. But who knows which guard. However the job gets done, Chismoso is more reliable than a weather vane.

From where Santiago stands with his fingers laced through the chain-link fence in the outdoor area, no bus is visible in the parking lot. But tomorrow . . .

"How badly do you want to know?" Chismoso grins, leaning his back against the fence Santiago grips.

"Forget it. Forget I asked." Santiago walks away, shoving his hands in the pockets stuffed with his metallic blanket, toothbrush, and mitten socks.

"According to a little bird I know"—Chismoso baits him—"the officials made contact with a woman called Agracia Reyes de la Luz."

Santiago stops cold, his heart racing. He can't believe it. That woman has no telephone, no actual address, and yet they've found her. Eyes narrowed, he turns slowly back to Chismoso.

"Looks like you've heard of her." Chismoso strolls toward him, arms swinging casually. From across the yard, Sumo raises his eyebrow. Santiago shakes his head. This he has to do alone.

"You're incorrect. I don't know anyone by that name." Santiago's lips barely move. The rest of him can't either.

"Really? Isn't she your *abuela*?"

A muscle in Santiago's neck twitches. "No, I don't have a grandmother."

"Interesting. She tried to deny knowing you, as well," Chismoso mocks.

A spark of hope. If she claims not to know him, then he can't be sent back to live with a "stranger."

"But when they threatened her, she admitted being related to you," Chismoso sneers.

Fine, so not the best news. What is Chismoso's point? What does he gain from all this? He's just a nobody.

"She'll take you," Chismoso says in one last stabbing remark. "Even though she wishes you were never born, Santi."

Santiago gives the gossiper a cold stare. The center has made him hard, and Chismoso himself taught him how to inflict pain. "But at least I have family willing to take me. And my name is Santiago."

Yes, she'll take him. Especially if officials threaten her. She'll complete her duty, as much as he wishes she wouldn't. He thought he would never have anything to do with that woman ever again. Except now that she's been located, he'll have to soon enough.

Soon enough comes the next day. The outside temperature matches the inside one. Santiago shuts his eyes, leaning into the fence and enjoying the sun warming his back. He hears, or rather feels, the bus's vibrations before it drives into the parking area. He cracks one eye open. *Sí,* there it is. A white bus, but other than that, completely nondescript.

The guards let them spend their whole recess outside, and when they return indoors, there's no list of boys to line up for the bus. Santiago saw the bus, heard it. So why's everything going on like a regular day? And if it is a regular day, why's his stomach aching with nerves and fear?

"García?" Castillo calls out after a few minutes.

Santiago refuses to look up from his book. It's not for him. At least two other Garcías reside in their area at the moment. If he ignores the guard, he'll go away.

"García Reyes?"

Slowly Santiago stands, his finger marking the page of his book he knows by heart.

"Leave the book behind," Castillo says.

What? No! Santiago grips his book, Mami's book, tighter.

"Señor Dante gave me this book—*gave* it to me," he stammers. A total lie. The book was donated to the center, and Señor Dante had nothing to do with the donations. But . . . "It's mine—I have to take it with me."

"No, everything that comes in belongs to the facility," Castillo says. And Santiago always thought of him as the "nice" guard.

He could refuse. Refuse to give up the book, refuse to leave the center. Except they would drag him out anyway. After taking away his book.

He removes his finger marking the page where he stopped and strokes the cover one last time. The edges firmed up a bit after that day in the rain but are still fatter than normal. The spine also shows signs of having been opened too many times. He traces the title written in wind puffs. Just as well. At least here someone else might enjoy it. At *la malvada*'s house it would only be used to feed the fire.

He turns to Pablo—both he and Sumo came to his side when Castillo called him—and hands him the book. "The little kids like it when you howl like the wind and make special voices for the other characters."

Pablo accepts the book with a nod. Santiago then turns to Sumo, who's lost some weight but looks more deflated than healthy. With his back to Castillo, he offers the big guy his hand. Sumo's eyes widen as Santiago inconspicuously passes him a packet of (wheat-free) fruit gummies in the handshake.

"Take care of yourself," Santiago says as Sumo quickly shoves his hand into his pocket. He also hands over his toothbrush. According to Chismoso, the center might stop handing out toothbrushes to newcomers, claiming it as an "unnecessary expense." Better someone use it than it getting thrown away.

Santiago retreats, unable to look at them anymore. Every time he makes friends, he loses them.

He takes in the main room once more. Cold, noisy,

crowded, confining, but still his home. Still better than what he has to look forward to. The door to the classroom, which opened so many opportunities, now stands perpetually closed and locked. If only he could say good-bye to Señor Dante.

On the plus side, there's the surprised expression on Chismoso's face. For once something is happening without his knowledge. *Take that,* Santiago thinks.

Castillo leads him down the hall and through the windowed door to the same holding room he'd been in so many months ago. In his hands, the guard places a plastic bag holding the clothes he'd worn when he arrived.

Despite the center's fear of vermin and disease, no one bothered to wash his clothes. The smell they give off from having been sealed in a plastic bag can knock down an army. Body odor, foot odor, dust, blood.

And the faintest hint of fruity shampoo.

He airs them out with a few good shakes. But the odors linger.

The jeans barely fasten at his waist and stop well above his ankles. The T-shirt fits fine, but that's the one with the strongest shampoo scent. If only he could find out if she's okay, then the memory wouldn't hurt so much. He shakes the shirt vigorously, turns it inside out, and puts it back on. With any luck, the scent will disappear quickly.

Something crinkles when he pulls on his socks. Too

flat to be a cockroach, but probably something just as sinister. Another shake and out comes the twenty-dollar bill Don José gave him before he left Capaz. He thought he'd lost it. It goes back in the sock before he puts it on.

The shoes have been stripped of their laces. Had he done that in his delusional, heatstroke state? He can't remember. But even without the laces, the shoes don't fit at all, and not just because his feet have gotten used to socks and flip-flops; his toes curl under completely. Despite the blazing, mountainous trek, at least the shoes are in decent condition. When he gets back to México, he'll go to the market and see if he can exchange these shoes for a larger, secondhand pair. Without laces, though, he won't get a good price. Why had he gotten rid of the laces?

He hands his facility clothes to Castillo along with his metallic blanket.

"Where are the others?" Santiago stops. No one else waits in the holding room.

"¿Cuáles otros?"

"The others riding the bus back to México?"

"You're not on the bus. Your family came for you."

Santiago trips on his too-small shoes. No, she didn't. She must have known that if he went back by bus, he'd make a run for it at the first stop. He'd run right now if his shoes weren't so small.

Only, she wouldn't have come herself—spend money to travel all this way on a bus? No, someone else got bullied to come instead. Maybe Tía Roberta, except who's looking after the kids? Tío Ysidro surely can't. Then it must be Tío Bernardo, Santiago's drunk uncle. It surprises Santiago that *la malvada* trusted him to make it to the center. The Tío Bernardo he knows would have disappeared into the wind as soon as he managed to cross the border. Guess things change.

They make him pass through the same metal detector he went through upon arrival. Did they think he'd try to steal one of those cozy metallic sheets? A guard he doesn't know hands him a clear plastic bag with his possessions. Except his pocketknife and Domínguez's lighter are missing. He definitely hadn't lost those on the journey—he remembers the metal detector beeping on arrival.

"*Con permiso,*" he says to this unfamiliar guard. "I'm missing some of my stuff."

The guard shakes his head. "Nothing that can be used as a weapon gets returned."

That explains the missing shoelaces. Great. Not only do they return people to their countries, they return them worse off than when they left.

All that's left in the plastic bag is the peso coin. And the triangular black lava stone he forgot to return to María Dolores, not that he believed her when she said it meant something to her. He shoves the worthless coin into his pocket.

The stone he'll toss once he gets outside. The burden of it is too much to carry. For a few more seconds, though, he keeps it in his hand, twirling it between his fingers until a shout causes him to drop it.

"Hey! You still have my family's heart stone!"

CHAPTER 40

The world stops. Nothing makes sense. It's a dream.

This woman has dark hair and long blond bangs that almost cover one eye. She wears stylish knockoff jeans, a striped blouse with fancy buttons set diagonally across the front, and a light jacket. She rushes forward with open arms, which he evades.

No touching.

"You don't seem happy to see me," María Dolores says, stopping half a meter away.

Santiago blinks. Happy? Yes, he's pleased she's not *la malvada* or any other blood relative. But full happiness? That'll take a while. Maybe once he can move again. "Of course I'm glad you're here. Just surprised." And confused, and a million other emotions he doesn't understand.

She crouches on the floor until she spots the lava stone he dropped. She flips it over, caressing its smooth edges. "I can't believe you kept my stone through everything."

"They only just returned it to me." No point saying he'd forgotten about it until a moment ago.

"Do you want to keep holding on to it for me?" she asks, her hand outstretched with it in her palm.

"Not really."

Her large eyes widen as if he slapped her.

"García, do you know this woman?" The same female guard who took his name and fingerprints when he arrived steps out from behind the desk. This is too much. Now the guards are sympathetic and cautious?

"Yes," he says, and because the guard continues to wait, he adds, "She's María Dolores Piedra Reyes."

"What's her relationship to you?" the guard asks.

He looks into María Dolores's wide, dark eyes. They remind him so much of Alegría's. Consuelo was wrong, though; he doesn't have their eyes. He turns his gaze back to the guard before answering the question. "She's my sister."

The guard's own eyes shift between the two of them. "Are you afraid of leaving with her?"

Afraid? He's more than a head taller than her. And after six months in a youth immigration detention center among teenage boys, he can, more than ever, take care of himself. But would his response really affect his release? If *la malvada* had come, could he have refused to leave with her? He wouldn't have thought so.

"I'm not scared, just surprised. It's fine, we're good. I can go?"

"You're free."

He and María Dolores remain glued to their spots a few seconds longer before their feet pry themselves from the floor, and they head out the glass front doors. He lifts his feet carefully to compensate for his curled toes and missing laces. Once outside, the spring air bites into his bare arms. Neither says anything as they head to an old blue car parked near the ominous white bus.

As he passes the bus, he gives it a hard stare. *I win.*

Then a blur of black pigtails and wide, bright eyes crashes into him.

"Santi!"

He catches Alegría in his arms and holds her tight as she locks her feet around his waist. His nose buries into her fruity-smelling hair; different, but nice. She's here; she's all right. How he missed her. His eyes begin to sting. No, he can't. Not here, not now.

He eases his grip to let her go, but she holds on tight with her legs and keeps her arms around his neck. She leans out to gaze at him.

"You look different, Santi," she says.

The sound of her nickname for him gives him a

twinge. After months of cringing every time someone said that name, it now makes his eyes sting again.

"Your hair is long enough to make pigtails," she continues.

"Yeah, I guess." Okay, a small smile won't kill him. He runs the free hand through his thick wavy hair he'd allowed to grow out. The facility brought in a barber every so often, but Santiago always refused. After his *tíos* shaved his head, having long hair felt like a rebellion and one of the few things he could control.

"Did you get my drawing?"

Her family portrait Consuelo delivered. The one he threw away when he thought they'd abandoned him, then instantly regretted. Darn eyes, he must have allergies. "It was beautiful."

"And guess what? Princesa came back. She was just looking after Mami. She's okay now."

From the driver's side of the car, another woman emerges. Plump with black hair pulled into a short ponytail; wide, near-black eyes; and a huge smile. If he had seen her first, he would have mistaken her for her sister. "Hi, I'm María Eugenia, your other sister."

He accepts her traditional kiss in greeting. "Thank you for driving out to get me."

"Of course. So great to finally meet you." María Eugenia gestures to the car. "Let's get out of here. I've got a tray of enchiladas *suizas* that needs to go in the oven."

¡Qué delicia! María Dolores mouths. Santiago says nothing.

He sits in the back seat with Alegría while the women sit in the front. Alegría slips her hand into his as they drive through the open gates of the facility. Once clear, he lets out a huge breath. Last time he tried to get through, the gates slammed in his face. For better or worse, the center became his home, a place where he knew the routine, knew what to expect. If anything, he'll miss that.

The landscape remains the same parched tan-brown he remembers from their trek, with no signs of other buildings or roads. In the far distance, a long range of rolling foothills peak into mountains. If those are part of the same mountain range they crossed, he can't imagine how they made it as far as they did.

Signs of civilization start cropping up with other cars and wider roads, while cattle graze on either side of the highway. A half hour later they stop in a small town with nothing more than a dozen buildings, pulling into a gas station.

"Maji," María Dolores tells her sister as they all get out of the car. "Can you take Alegría to the bathroom while I fill up?"

"But I don't need to go," Alegría protests.

María Dolores shakes her head. "I want you to try anyway."

"Can Santi come with us?"

"No, *mamita*, I need him for something here," she says.

María Eugenia grabs Alegría's hand. "After we pee, we'll get some snacks."

María Dolores places the nozzle into the tank before turning to Santiago with her hands on her hips. "Talk to me. What is your problem?"

Under the shade next to the pumps, the temperature drops. Santiago tries to shove his hands into his pockets, but they don't fit. He folds his arms across his chest and leans against the car. He doesn't want to hear it. He scuffs his too-small shoe against the pavement. "Nothing."

Pointing a finger at his face, she forces him to make eye contact. "I told you once before, I don't appreciate people lying to me."

They stare at each other for a few seconds until Santiago's shoulders slump and his eyes drop.

"I thought you were dead," he whispers. "When they took you away."

"I almost was." She nods. "Another hour and I would have been. They kept me in the intensive care unit for three days."

Now his voice hardens as he crosses his arms tighter. "But they didn't detain you? They took Alegría away from me. I worried she'd died too. I stole food for a guy to get information about her. He said she'd left with her family. How did you manage that?"

María Dolores sighs. "My brother-in-law's friend is a pastor who runs a church refuge. He made the arrangements so I wouldn't be detained and helped get Alegría out as well. We still have court dates, though. Who knows if they'll grant us the asylum we requested."

"But you didn't come for me." He kicks the car tire with the sole of his foot before remembering his curled-under toes. Pain inside, pain outside. "I wrote millions of letters to get into foster care. I filled out applications so I wouldn't have to live behind a fence topped with razor wire. I helped the obnoxious guards. I saved your life, and your daughter's, and you forgot all about me."

"Of course I didn't forget about you." She throws her arms up in the air. "I'm here, aren't I?"

"Six months later!"

"That's how long it took to get a copy of your birth certificate. They wouldn't release you to me unless I could prove we were related."

All defenses drop. His voice returns to a whisper. "You got my birth certificate?"

María Dolores reaches in through the open car window and extracts a clear plastic folder with a piece of paper inside. The Mexican seal on the left, Chihuahuan seal on the right. Below the two seals, he reads the words:

ACTA DE NACIMIENTO
NOMBRES: Santiago García Reyes

"It says my birthday is the twenty-third of March?" No one ever bothered telling him that.

María Dolores smiles a little. "Which is in a few days. Alegría wants to throw you a unicorn party."

He keeps on reading.

NOMBRE DEL PADRE: Juan García García

A name so common that it could be almost anyone.

NOMBRE DE LA MADRE: Sofinda Reyes de la Luz

Here, in his hands, is proof that Mami really existed, and that she had been his *mamá*.

"How did you manage to get this?" His eyes refuse to leave the paper, taking in every detail. His time of birth is 14:16; his mother had been twenty years old when she had him.

"Trust me, it wasn't easy." María Dolores moves closer to him. "Six months of phone calls and letters, getting archives of Chihuahuan newspapers in search of birth announcements, filing paperwork, a few bribes to the right people. Every time I got close, something else would set me back. Luckily, I don't give up easily."

The gas pump pops to indicate a full tank, but neither removes it.

He can't believe it. That she went through all of that. For him. "I wish I'd known."

She turns in surprise to look at him. "But I wrote about this in the letters. Almost every week. I thought maybe you didn't know how to read but figured someone could read them to you."

"I can read now, but I never got any letters. None of us did."

"Oh, that explains so much." She places a hand on his arm. This time he doesn't flinch or shake it off. "But even when you thought we'd forgotten you, you still told them we were your sisters. Me and Alegría. *La guardia* had that on file. Knew who I was when I showed my identification."

Yes, he did say that. "I tried to exclude that information, but the word *hermanas* kept coming out."

"You saved our lives. I could never stop thinking about you as my *hermano*. No matter what happens, we're in this together."

Her words make him smile like never before. "Thank you, my sister."

She throws her arms around him in a tight hug, standing on her toes in order to reach. He lets her, doesn't pull away. More comfort, more security. Now if asked, he remembers what happy feels like.

"Damn you for growing so tall," she says, finally easing herself away and fussing over the wet spot she left on his shirt. "And you're still way too skinny. But why is your shirt inside out?"

He laughs. How long since he did that? "Doesn't matter anymore."

"Santi, guess what!" Alegría bounces out of the convenience store. "They have raspberry ice creams. Do you want one?"

"Of course." Even with the chill, how can he say no? He turns to María Dolores. "Can I buy her one? Is twenty dollars enough?"

"Should be enough to buy several."

"¿Cuatro?"

She grins. "Probably. But can I have a chocolate one instead?"

"Anything you want." He swoops down for Alegría and swings her up to sit on his shoulders.

"Again, again!" she screeches, but he holds on tight to her ankles, not wanting to let her go, and turns to the other sister instead.

"María Eugenia, what kind of ice cream do you like?"

"Chocolate, of course."

He reminds Alegría to duck as they enter through the

doorway of the convenience store. The variety in the ice cream chest is unbelievable. Someday, when he can read the different English flavors, he'll try them all.

Next to the ice cream chest, a rickety rack holds postcards showing the beauty and diversity beyond the dry, harsh New Mexican desert. If two raspberry ice creams cost $3.50 apiece, and the two chocolate ones are $3.99 each, he still has plenty to get some postcards at $0.99. One to send to Don José in Capaz, because he promised. Another for Consuelo from both him and Alegría. And one to write to Señor Dante. Because, thanks to him, he can.

Back in the car, ice creams long gone (though Alegría still sports a handsome red mustache), a loud thundercloud rumbles in the distance. Alegría leans as close to Santiago as her seat belt allows.

"I don't like thunder, Santi," she says.

"Can I tell you a story?" he asks. Alegría nods against his shoulder.

His fingers absently run through her thick pigtails. "When I was your age, I was scared of thunder too. Until my *mami* said that thunder is like a drum, announcing the arrival of rain. Rain is what makes things grow and also washes away what isn't wanted, leaving a fresh start."

"But why do the thunder and rain have to be so loud?" Alegría asks.

"Because it's a party, a celebration. Mami and I used to

sing and dance in the rain. She said it honored the rain to feel the drops on our skin instead of hiding from it. When we embrace the rain, she said, we're free."

Alegría snuggles closer. "Can we do that too? Dance in the rain?"

Santiago's hand drops from her pigtails. As much as he tries to stop them, memories prey on his heart: His *tía* criticizing him for letting her kids play in the mud, and *la malvada* insulting him and his *mami*; the one time in the center where he got soaked to the core and almost died.

No, he won't let those thoughts ruin things. Not anymore. "I'd like that. Dancing together will be a *tremenda fiesta*." Santiago kisses the top of Alegría's head. "If your *mami* says it's okay. And if there's a way to get dry and warm afterward."

María Dolores turns around from the front seat and grabs Santiago's hand, giving it a squeeze. "Of course, to all of that. But only if I can party in the rain with *ustedes*."

"Me too!" María Eugenia says from the driver seat.

Another clap of thunder rattles the car. This time, Alegría sits up. "Do you think it'll rain when we get home?"

Santiago gazes out the window. The sun behind the thunderclouds has caused them to turn brilliant shades of purple and pink.

Home, a future he's never known.

"Yes, *creo que sí*."

AUTHOR'S NOTE

At the time of writing this, hundreds of people are trying to enter the U.S. daily. Holding centers are well exceeding capacity, and cities near the border struggle to provide resources for the influx of refugees. Laws continuously change, and yet little, if anything, seems to be done to improve the lives of those held in custody. Even the deaths of several children while in these holding facilities hasn't (to my knowledge) resulted in any progressive change in the situation. Newspapers report that it costs over seven hundred dollars per person, per day, to house the youths in immigration centers, and the government claims there's not enough funding to provide better living conditions. Wherever all this money goes, it's not benefiting any immigrant or refugee.

Even though Santiago's story is a work of fiction, as is

the facility where he's detained, most of his experiences are true to past and current immigration hardships. They were taken from various accounts of youths and adults held at both temporary and long-term facilities throughout the country. A lot of children who are currently entering the U.S. are kept in far worse conditions than Santiago faced: often denied access to sufficient and clean water and food, crammed together in large "cages," and don't provide toothbrushes and soap or medical attention. Providing education, which a few years ago had been obligatory, has almost completely vanished from centers, and yet the government expects the youths to learn English.

Some children are still being taken from their parents; a lawyer friend really did deliver breast milk for a baby separated from her mother. Belts and shoelaces are removed from the detainees, along with anything else perceived as dangerous, leaving them worse off than they were before their arrival. A lot of youths entering the U.S. today turn themselves in at the border as they seek asylum, while others still try to enter the country illegally.

Due to the remoteness, some people attempt to cross the desert border running through New Mexico, Arizona, and California, not realizing the natural challenges they must endure. In an ideal world a person would have one to two gallons of water per day of desert crossing—a very heavy task, considering how much water weighs. There are accounts of people dying only a few hours after their vehicle left them stranded. Likewise, there are reports of people surviving four to five days of intense desert temperatures reaching well over one hundred degrees Fahrenheit, and having run out of water days before. Sometimes helpful citizens will leave bottles of water under a bush for immigrants to drink, while others deliberately destroy the water supply to prevent immigration. Unfortunately, hundreds of people die each year trying to cross the desert, and there are many more whose remains are never found. Despite the extreme hardships people go through to immigrate to the U.S., and then the further hardships faced once here, thousands of youths risk everything to live here. Severe gang violence in their hometowns has them running literally for their lives. For others, poverty is a factor leading to immigration. For example, the current daily wage in Mexico is about five U.S. dollars (https://www .hklaw.com/en/insights/publications/2018/12/mexico -to-increase-minimum-wage-for-2019). Several children, like Santiago, are also escaping abusive relatives. The emotional impact of this book made it a challenge to write. It's heart-wrenching to learn what extremes refugees are forced into when they attempt to reach safety or seek asylum. But at the same time, I knew I had to write Santiago's story. Without awareness, nothing changes. Here's the awareness, now let's bring forth the change.

—A. D.

Resources

American Academy of Pediatrics. "American Academy of Pediatrics Urges Compassion and Appropriate Care for Immigrant and Refugee Children." March 13, 2017. https://www.aap.org/en-us/about-the-aap/aap-press-room/pages/american-academy-of-pediatrics-urges-compassion-and-appropriate-care-for-immigrant-and-refugee-children.aspx. Arnold, Amanda. "What to Know About the Detention Centers for Immigrant Children Along the U.S.–Mexico Border." *The Cut*, June 21, 2018. https://www.thecut.com/2018/06/immigrant-children-detention-center-separated-parents.html.

Barry, Dan, et al. "Migrant Children Tell of Life Without Parents Inside US Immigration Detention Centres." *Independent*, July 16, 2018. https://www.independent.co.uk/news/world/americas/migrant-children-us-immigration-centres-family-separation-a8449276.html.

Bogado, Aura. "ICE Isn't Following Its Own Handbook on How to Deport Kids." PRI, April 25, 2018. https://www.pri.org/stories/2018-04-25/ice-isn-t-following-its-own-handbook-how-deport-kids.

Button, Liz. "ABA to Collect Books at Winter Institute 14 for Refugees at the Southern U.S. Border." American Booksellers Association, November 18, 2018. https://www.bookweb.org/news/aba-collect -books-winter-institute-14-refugees-southern -us-border-108586.

Chapin, Angelina. "Drinking Toilet Water, Widespread Abuse: Report Details 'Torture' For Child Detainees." *Huffpost*, last modified July 18, 2018. https:// www.huffpost.com/entry/migrant-children-detail -experiences-border-patrol-stations-detention-centers _n_5b4d13ffe4b0de86f485ade8.

Cooper, Nicole. Lecture at the University of the Incarnate Word, San Antonio, TX, November 6, 2017.

Cotter, Holland. "For Migrants Headed North, the Things They Carried to the End." *New York Times*, March 3, 2017. https://www.nytimes.com/2017/03/03/arts /design/state-of-exception-estado-de-excepcion -parsons-mexican-immigration.html.

Dickson, Caitlin. "'I Thought I Would Never See Him': Asylum Seeker and Son Reunite After Border

Separation." Yahoo News, July 17, 2018. https://www
.yahoo.com/news/thought-never-see-asylum-seeker
-son-reunite-border-separation-163945092.html.

Dickerson, Caitlin. "Detention of Migrant Children
Has Skyrocketed to Highest Levels Ever." *New York
Times*, September 12, 2018. https://www.nytimes
.com/2018/09/12/us/migrant-children-detention.html.

Garcia Bochenek, Michael. "No Way to Treat Children Fleeing Danger." *Harvard International Review*, July 26, 2018.

Gómez, Grace. Immigration lawyer. http://www
.gomezimmigration.com/.

Hlavinka, Elizabeth. "UT Immigration Clinic Lawyers Rep-
resent Detained Immigrant Women, Children." *The Daily
Texan*, February 11, 2016. http://www.dailytexanonline
.com/2016/02/11/ut-immigration-clinic-lawyers
-represent-detained-immigrant-women-children.

Huang, Wen. "Q&A on Child Immigration Crisis
with Law School's Maria Woltjen." *UChicago News*,
July 14, 2014. https://news.uchicago.edu/story/qa
-child-immigration-crisis-law-schools-maria-woltjen.

International Rescue Committee. "What's in My Bag? What Refugees Bring When They Run for Their Lives." *Medium*, September 4, 2015. https://medium .com/uprooted/what-s-in-my-bag-758d435f6e62.

Office of Refugee Resettlement. https://www.acf.hhs .gov/orr.

Sharp, Jay W. "Water, Water . . . Nowhere: Survival in the Desert." DesertUSA. https://www.desertusa.com /desert-activity/thirst.html.

Stillman, Sarah. "The Five-Year-Old Who Was Detained at the Border and Persuaded to Sign Away Her Rights." *The New Yorker*, October 11, 2018. https://www .newyorker.com/news/news-desk/the-five-year-old -who-was-detained-at-the-border-and-convinced-to -sign-away-her-rights.

Taxin, Amy. "Immigrant Children Describe Treatment in Detention Centers." AP News, July 18, 2018. https://www .apnews.com/1a8db84a88a940049558b4c450dccc8a.

Urrea, Luis Alberto. *The Devil's Highway: A True Story.* New York: Hachette, 2005.

Further Reading

Picture Books

Agee, Jon. *The Wall in the Middle of the Book*. New York: Dial Books for Young Readers, 2018.

Buitrago, Jairo and Rafael Yockteng. *Two White Rabbits*. Toronto: Groundwood Books, 2015.

Danticat, Edwidge. *Mama's Nightingale: A Story of Immigration and Separation*. New York: Dial Books for Young Readers, 2015.

Mills, Deborah. *La Frontera: El viaje con papá/My Journey with Papa*. Cambridge, MA: Barefoot Books, 2018.

Morales, Yuyi. *Dreamers*. New York: Neal Porter Books, 2018.

Surat, Michele Maria. *Angel Child, Dragon Child*. New York: Scholastic, 1989.

Tonatiuh, Duncan. *Pancho Rabbit and the Coyote: A Migrant's Tale*. New York: Abrams, 2013.

Middle-Grade

Bausum, Ann. *Denied, Detained, Deported: Stories from the Dark Side of American Immigration*. Washington, DC: National Geographic Children's Books, 2009.

Colfer, Eoin and Andrew Donkin. *Illegal*. Naperville, IL: Sourcebooks Jabberwocky, 2018.

Park, Linda Sue. *A Long Walk to Water: Based on a True Story*. Boston: HMH Books for Young Readers, 2011.

Senzai, N. H. *Shooting Kabul*. New York: Simon & Schuster Books for Young Readers, 2010.

Young Adults

Clark, Tea Rozman, ed. *Green Card Youth Voices* series. Green Card Youth Voices, various.

Marquardt, Marie. *The Radius of Us*. New York: St. Martin's Griffin, 2017.

Schafer, Steve. *The Border*. Naperville, IL: Sourcebooks Fire, 2016.

Zoboi, Ibi. *American Street*. New York: Balzer + Bray, 2017.

Adults

De León, Jason. *The Land of Open Graves: Living and Dying on the Migrant Trail*. Oakland: University of California Press, 2015.

Patel, Lisa (Leigh). *Youth Held at the Border: Immigration, Education, and the Politics of Inclusion*. New York: Teachers College Press, 2013.

Regan, Margaret. *Detained and Deported: Stories of Immigrant Families Under Fire*. Boston: Beacon Press, 2015.

Glossary

Compared to other languages, Spanish is fairly easy to read. It is a phonetic language, meaning that things are pronounced as they're written, but keep in mind that some letters are pronounced differently in Spanish than in English. Vowels, for example, are pronounced ah, eh, ee, oh, oo (A, E, I, O, U). Try sounding out some of these words and see if you can figure out what they mean before reading the definition. (Some will be easier than others!)

A gloria: something that tastes "delicious" tastes *a gloria*.

A toda fuerza: "by force," as in "I will separate you by force."

Abuelo/abuela/abuelita: grandfather, grandmother, granny.

Acento: "accent," as in speaking with one.

Acta de nacimiento: birth certificate.

Acuéstate: the order to "lie down" (go to sleep).

Adoptar: this word means both "to adopt" and "to foster."

Ahora: now.

Alé, alé: a phrase probably taken from French (*allez, allez*), it means "go, go" or "hurry."

Alegre: happy.

Alegría: a woman's name that also means "joy."

Alegría, te quiero. Tu hermano, Santiago: Alegría, I love you. Your brother, Santiago.

Almohadas: "pillows," which, unfortunately, most immigration centers don't provide.

Alto: a command to "stop."

Arroz con pollo: a common and easy meal, "rice with chicken."

Ay: a word with multiple meanings, depending on the intonation used. Similar to "oh."

Ay, cariño: a term of endearment, similar to "oh, sweetie."

Ay, qué rico: usually used to indicate something feeling or tasting nice, "ah, that's good."

Ay, perdóneme: an apology, "oh, excuse me" or "sorry."

Basta: usually used as a command to mean "stop it," or "enough."

Bróder: a Spanish attempt to say "brother" in the way people call buddies or those of the same background "brother."

Bueno: usually means "good" but can also mean "okay" or "well then" before continuing with what one was saying.

Buenos días, chicos: Good morning, kids.

Burro: "donkey," which can also be used in English!

Caballo: horse.

Café con leche: coffee with milk.

Cállate ya: a command to be quiet, "shut up now."

Calle: road, street.

Cállense: a command to tell a group to "shut up" or "be quiet."

Cantina: a place that serves food and drinks.

Capaz: A fictional village on the Mexican border with New Mexico. Literally meaning "capable," but it can easily become *incapaz*, making it "incapable."

Caramelos: literally means "caramels" but can also be "candy."

Catorce: fourteen.

Centavos: Mexican "cents," which are virtually worthless, and many vendors will round up to the nearest peso instead of giving you that change.

Chicharrones: "pork rinds," often sold in bags, like potato chips.

Chicos, vamos: Kids, let's go.

Chiquitin/chiquitines: little one, young 'uns.

Chismoso: someone who gossips.

Chulo malcriado: the word *chulo* has different meanings depending where you're from. In this case it means a "moocher" (someone who lives off other peoples' money). *Malcriado* literally means "poorly raised" or "ill bred."

Cien: one hundred.

Claro: "sure" or "of course."

Claro que no: of course not.

Claro que sí: a more emphatic "of course."

Claro, hijo: Sure, son.

Como dicen en inglés: As they say in English.

Compañeros: literally means "companions" but more often used for "schoolmates" or, as in Santiago's case, "fellow detainees."

Con permiso: "excuse me," whether interrupting, asking for permission, or apologizing.

Coyote: technically it's an animal, cousin to dogs and foxes, but it's also the term for the people who smuggle immigrants into the U.S.

Creo que sí: I think so.

¿Cuáles otros?: Which others?

Cuatro: four.

Dale, caballito: the equivalent of "giddyup," literally means "c'mon, horsey."

De lo más bien: in this book's context it's "just fine," but in other settings it can be "really good."

De nada: reply to *gracias*, "you're welcome."

Desgraciado: literally means "disgraceful," as in someone people are ashamed of.

Dije que no: I said no.

Don: a word of respect for a man.

¿Dónde está?: Where is she/he/it?

¿Dónde estoy?: Where am I?

El caballo entero: literally means "the whole horse" but is also a word for "stallion."

El campo: "the country" or "the countryside."

El cocinero: the cook.

El conejo corre / En su hueco se esconde / Así el coyote / No se lo come: a poem I made up to be recited while tying shoes. The literal translation is: "The rabbit runs / In his hole he hides / That way the coyote / Doesn't eat him." In Spanish it does kind of rhyme!

El Norte: literally means "the north" but used as a nickname for the U.S.

El otro lado: literally means "the other side" but is used in Mexico to signify the U.S. (the other side of the border).

El viejo: the old man.

En español: in Spanish.

Entren ahora: an order to a group to "enter now" or "come in now."

Está bien: "it's okay" or "it's all right."

Está . . . se: the start of two questions, "Is . . . did."

Estado de Chihuahua: did you know Mexico has states

(estados) just like the U.S.? Chihuahua is both a city and a state in northern Mexico.

Este tipo: "this guy" or "this dude."

Ey: a slang word for "yes," similar to "yeah."

Favor: in this instance it's short for *por favor*, "please."

Frambuesa: raspberry.

Fuego: fire.

Fulano: a word that means "somebody" or "anybody," often used when you don't know the specific person's name.

Gacho: a person who is "worthless" or a "lowlife."

Gracias: if you learn only one word in Spanish, learn this one! "Thank you."

Guanaco: an offensive word to call someone from El Salvador. Santiago's friend chose not to let the word hurt him but to own it.

Guardia: a female "guard."

Hermano/hermana/hermanito: "brother," "sister," and "little brother," usually reserved for people who are related (not just a buddy).

Hija: daughter.

Hijos: could be "sons" or "sons and daughters." Some people will also use "hijo" or "hija" as a term of endearment even if they're not related.

Hola: pronounced "oh-la," it's good to know how to say "hi."

Hombre: a "man," can also be used when addressing a friend like, "Hey, man."

Huérfano: an "orphan," like Santiago.

Idiota: an "idiot," can be used for both males and females.

Imbécil: imbecile.

La malvada: this is the nickname Santiago uses for his abusive grandmother, meaning "the evil one."

La migra: a nickname for the immigration officers who patrol near the border.

La princesa y el viento: *The Princess and the Wind*, a fictional picture book that Santiago's *mami* used to read to him when he was young.

Ladrones: "thieves" or "robbers."

Lárgate: a command to "leave" or "get lost."

Lentejo: Mexican slang for someone who's slow and stupid.

Levántate: a command to "wake up" or "get up."

Ley Unido: while this is a fictional organization (meaning "Law United"), there are several pro-bono law firms and nonprofits that help youths and families in the holding centers.

Listo: a word with multiple meanings, it can be "ready" and also "smart/sharp-witted."

Llama al médico: Call the doctor/medic.

Llorón: "crier" or "crybaby," but can also be used for someone who "whines" a lot.

Lo siento: a sympathetic phrase you'd say if you feel bad for someone, "I'm sorry."

Loco: crazy.

Los azules: literally means "the blues," but near the border it's a colloquial Mexican term for police officers from the U.S., due to their blue (*azul*) uniforms.

Madre e hija: mother and daughter.

Madre soltera: single mom.

Malcriado: someone who is ill-mannered and/or poorly behaved, could also be a "brat."

Mamis: mommies.

Mamita: a term of endearment, often said to a little girl, similar to "sweetie."

Mano: short for hermano ("brother"), and used to address a buddy or "bro."

Manzano: a play on words. Literally means "apple tree," but in this case it's "apple boy."

Me lo prometes: Do you promise me?

Medio mundo: an exaggeration and expression meaning "half the world," similar to the English expression "everyone and his uncle."

Mentira: a lie.

Menudo: a Mexican stew made out of tripe. (The word also has several different meanings depending where you use it and the context.)

Mi hermana: my sister.

Mi nombre es Santiago: My name is Santiago.

Mi'jo: a contraction of "mi hijo" ("my son") and used as a form of endearment, especially by an older person to a younger person.

Mira: literally means "look," but can also mean "hey."

Mosca: "fly" or "bug."

Muchísimas gracias: thank you very much.

Muy bien: "very good" or even "all right."

Ni amor: nor love.

Niños y bebés: kids and babies.

No, al Polo Norte, idiota: a sarcastic response, "no, to the North Pole, idiot."

No es justo: It's not fair.

No tiene que hacer eso: a formal way to say "you don't have to do that."

Noche Buena: the word for "Christmas Eve," which most Latin Americans celebrate instead of Christmas Day. Literally, it means "night good."

Nombre de la madre: mother's name.

Nombre del padre: father's name.

Nombres: names (referring to first and middle names, or full name).

Nopales: the edible pads of some cactus plants, which can be bought in specialty stores. Do not harvest or eat them from the wild unless you know how to first get rid of the tiny glochids, or hairs, that will painfully embed into your hands and tongue!

O lo que sea: an off-handed expression that means "or whatever."

Ojos: eyes.

Oye: literally means "listen" or "hear," but often used as "hey."

Oye, chico: Hey, kid.

Oye, flaco: "Hey, slim/skinny." In Spanish it's common to have a nickname based on one's physical appearance.

Paletas: "ice cream bars" or "Popsicles."

"Pai" de calabaza: "pai" is not a Spanish word; it's an attempt to say "pie," which doesn't have a good Spanish equivalent. So this is "pumpkin pie" (pie of pumpkin).

Pare: a command to "stop."

Patas flacas: a mild insult that means "skinny legs," though in some countries the word "patas" is reserved for animal legs, so the insult could even be "skinny animal legs."

Pegado: a colloquial term for sticky, burned rice at the bottom of the pot. Some kids will demand and eat this in handheld chunks!

Pero desgraciadamente: but unfortunately.

¿Pero en inglés o en español?: But in English or Spanish?

Perro: normally, this is the word for "dog," but in the context used, it's a derogatory word for "policeman."

Peso: the monetary unit of Mexico, represented by the same symbol as the U.S. dollar ($). The current value is about nineteen Mexican pesos per U.S. dollar.

Pipí: "pee-pee" or "potty."

Pollos: generally refers to "chicken" used in food (but sometimes also the live animal); in this case it's the colloquial/ derogatory word used to refer to the people trying to cross the border.

Por favor: another word that will get you far, "please."

¿Por qué?: why?

Por persona: per person.

Posole: a side dish or stew made from maize (a starchy cousin of sweet corn).

Primos: cousins.

¿Qué?: As a question, it usually means "what?"

Qué delicia: "what a delicacy" or "how delicious."

Qué linda: "how pretty" or "what a pretty thing."

Qué locos desgraciados: in the context used, it's meaning is close to "what a bunch of disrespectful imbeciles/crazies."

¿Qué más?: What else?

Que no cumplió: referring to someone who didn't keep their end of a bargain.

Quiero a mi mamá: in the context used it's "I want my mom." But it can also be "I love my mom."

Rellenos: often refers to stuffed chile peppers, which are then dipped in batter and fried.

¿Sabe usted?: again using the formal "you," it means "do you know?"

Sabiondo: a "know-it-all."

Serpiente: serpent.

Sí: yes (note the accent mark on the *i*—without it the word becomes "if").

Sí, ahora: yes, now.

Sí, por favor: yes, please.

Sin apellidos: "without last names" or "no last names."

Sin vergüenzas: a mild insult, people who are without shame or remorse, "shameless."

Solo la niña: only the girl.

Sopa de pollo: chicken soup.

Soy: I am.

Suizas: "Swiss," in the book it refers to enchiladas *suizas*, which tend to have a cream sauce.

'Tá bien: an abbreviation for *"está bien,"* "it's okay" or "all right."

Tamal: the singular form for tamales, a corn-based dough with various fillings that is wrapped in corn husks or banana leaves and then steamed.

Tele: a short word for "television," similar to "TV."

Telenovelas: Spanish-language soap operas known for being overly dramatic.

Tía/tío/tíos: "aunt," "uncle," and "aunt and uncle."

Tiene movimiento: literally this means "has movement" but refers in this case to a road with traffic.

¿Tiene usted hermanos aquí también?: Do (formal) you have siblings here too?

Tienes razón: You're right.

Tome: the formal command for "here" or "take this."

Tremenda fiesta: a great party.

Tú: you (informal).

Tu madre: your mother.

Un chile de todos los moles: a Mexican expression indicating a "good egg," someone who's helpful and considerate. Literally translates to "a chile for all sauces."

Usted: the formal form for "you," often used to address an older person or to show respect to someone.

Ustedes: you all.

Ustedes dos: you two.

Vamos: Let's go.

Valle Cobre: a fictional mining village in southern New Mexico named "Copper Valley."

Ven: a command to "come" or "come here."

Veo una casa: I see a house.

Viejita: one word to signify "little old lady."

Vos: an informal form of "you" used in parts of Central America and Argentina but not often heard elsewhere.

Voy a salir: "I'm getting out" or "I'm leaving."

Y si no puedo: "And if I can't" or "And if I'm unable to."

Y yo: and me/I.

Ya sé: an emphasis on "I know," similar to "Yes, I know" or "I already know."

Ya vengo: I'm coming.

Zanate: a "grackle," a songbird common in Mexico.

A Reading Group Guide to
Santiago's Road Home
by Alexandra Diaz

About the Book

Fleeing a physically abusive home, twelve-year-old Santiago finds an unexpected family in María Dolores and her young daughter, Alegría. Together, they decide to make the dangerous journey across the border to *el otro lado*, the United States. The path is full of danger, but nothing prepares Santiago for what awaits him on the other side. *Santiago's Road Home* takes readers inside an ICE detention facility, shedding light on the challenges children like Santiago face, while affirming their resilience, strength, and determination to work hard for better lives.

Discussion Questions

1. A book's prologue is often used to establish setting and provide details that will connect to the main story. What questions about Santiago's story do you have after reading the prologue? As you read, try to find the answers to these questions. Which questions would you like more information about?

2. What do Santiago's memories of his mother reveal about her? Why do you think the memory of dancing in the rain made such an impression on him? What is your favorite memory of a loved one? How does reflecting on it make you feel?

3. Why does María Dolores decide to go to the United States? Why does Santiago ask to go with her? Why do you think María Dolores decides to let Santiago accompany them on the journey?

4. Describe María Dolores's plan for crossing the border into the United States. What is dangerous about this plan? Why do you think she does not try to immigrate legally? Why does Santiago remark later that "the possibility of [immigrating] the 'correct way' hadn't even occurred to him"?

5. María Dolores tells Santiago, "'Even though I don't have much, I like to support hardworking people trying to make a living.'" What does this statement reveal about her values and priorities? Explain your answer. What do you most value in your life? How do you act upon or share your values?

6. How does Santiago's willingness to work hard and help others allow him to gain the trust of those he

meets on his journey, such as Don José, Domínguez, Consuelo, and Señor Dante? How do these adults help him in return?

7. According to the glossary, *coyote* is a term for a person who smuggles immigrants into the United States. How does Santiago find a trustworthy coyote? What does Dominguez say about the difference between good coyotes and bad coyotes? Why do you think he considers what he does "an honest living," even though what he is doing is illegal?

8. Which part of Santiago's journey across the desert do you think was the most dangerous? Where do you see him having to be strong for others? When do you see others looking out for him? Explain your answers.

9. Describe Santiago's favorite childhood story: *La princesa y el viento.* What do you think is the moral of this story? Why do you think this particular story means so much to Santiago? What was your favorite fairy tale or folktale when you were younger? What did you like most about it?

10. When Santiago first sees the detention center, he notices that it "resembles a prison instead of a sanctuary." Later,

his friend Guanaco notes that children in detention "'have fewer rights than murderers.'" Describe the conditions in the detention center. How is it similar to and different from a prison? What kind of atmosphere does this create for the children inside?

11. How does learning to read and write impact Santiago's life? Señor Dante says that the government has decided to stop funding educational programs in detention centers because it is a "luxury they can no longer afford." Do you think that education is a luxury or a necessity? Do you think all children should have access to an education? Explain your answers.

12. Santiago, María Dolores, and Alegría claim that they are siblings even though they are not related by blood. What does Santiago mean when he says that admitting he has two sisters is "the internal truth"? Do you have people in your life who you consider to be family even though you are not related? What is your definition of family?

13. What does it mean for someone immigrating to be granted asylum? Why does Señora Bárbara say that Santiago has a great case for being granted asylum in the United States?

14. Señor Dante tells the boys in his class that even though they cannot control the future, they can control how they respond to what comes their way. How does Santiago demonstrate this ability to control how he responds to adversity? How could you apply this advice to your own life?

15. What makes Santiago think that María Dolores forgot about him? What does he find out to understand what really happened?

16. It is often possible to analyze a story as a hero's journey—a type of narrative with specific steps. One of these steps involves the hero being tested. How many different tests does Santiago face on his journey? Consider events that tested him physically and emotionally, as well as times when he had to use intelligence and creativity to solve a problem. What characteristics helped him overcome these challenges?

17. When we talk about words, we say that they have both denotative (literal) and connotative (associative) meanings. What are different meanings for the word *home*? What do you think the title *Santiago's Road Home* means?

18. Read the author's note and resources sections at the end of the novel. *Santiago's Road Home* is a work of fiction,

yet it is based on true accounts of people immigrating to the United States. Does knowing that information change the way you think about the story? Explain your answer. Why do you think the author, Alexandra Diaz, wrote this novel? What do you think she hopes readers will understand after reading it?

19. We discuss books about other cultural experiences as being either *mirrors* or *windows*. A mirror is a book that reflects your own experience in some way, allowing you to see a part of yourself in the story. A window is a book that allows you to look into the experience of someone whose life is very different from your own, and, as a result, helps you to understand things that others experience. Was this book a mirror or a window for you? Why do you think it is important to read both types of books?

Extension Activities

1. Consider the following comment from *Santiago's Road Home*: "Not playing by the rules didn't make someone bad. Especially if the rules were unjust to begin with." Do you believe that there are times when it is okay to break a rule or disobey a law? Write a persuasive essay or speech about whether or not you agree with this statement.

2. Reflect on your experience reading a book that uses vocabulary from two different languages. How often were you able to understand what unfamiliar words meant based on their contexts? How often did you need to refer to the glossary? Try writing a short story or short autobiography that incorporates words from another language. Try to provide enough context for a reader to comprehend the meaning of these words. At the end of the story, include a glossary. Exchange your story with a partner, and then discuss your experiences reading each other's work.

3. In chapter fourteen, the author reveals that both María Dolores and Santiago left Mexico to escape domestic violence. After spending time in the harsh detention center, Santiago thinks, "As horrible as staying here would be, it [doesn't] compare with returning back there." Research the reasons that people attempt to immigrate to the United States, especially women and children. What are the most common reasons? Are they similar to María Dolores's and Santiago's situations? Work in a small group to draft a proposal for measures that could help address one of the main reasons people like Santiago feel they have to leave their home countries.

4. María Dolores, Alegría, and Santiago almost die as a result of dehydration and heat stroke. Research the

dangers of dehydration and heat-related illnesses, and create an informative poster or video for your school about the importance of hydration. Think about the audience you'd like to reach, especially athletes and others who spend significant time outside.

5. In the detention center, Guanaco explains the separation policy to Santiago, saying, "'They say it's to keep people safe. Personally, I think it's to hold power. Only bullies separate you from your family.'" Research the government's separation policy for people immigrating to the United States. What reasons are given for separating adults from children and boys from girls? What reasons are given by advocates who oppose family separation policies? What do you think the government's policy *should* be? Explain your position using facts that you have researched from reliable sources.

6. Research the process for immigrating legally into the United States. Why is it difficult for someone in Santiago's position to follow this process? What role do nonprofits like Ley Unido play in helping people like Santiago enter the United States? As a class, come up with questions you have about the process or the history of immigration. Then decide who might be best to answer these questions, such as a local immigration

lawyer or advocacy group, and see if you can discuss with them via email or video conference.

7. One of the lawyers for Ley Unido tells Santiago, "'There are over thirteen thousand youths in facilities all over the country, and this is one of the better ones.'" Alexandra Diaz also references the fact that the United States government spends more than seven hundred dollars per person per day to hold children in immigration centers. If you were to design a facility that could house two hundred children awaiting immigration hearings at a cost of seven hundred dollars a day per person, what would be your monthly operating budget? How would you spend this budget? What programs and assistance would you provide for the children?

Guide prepared by Amy Jurskis,
English Department Chair at Oxbridge Academy.

If you liked *Santiago's Road Home*,
read on for a preview of *The Only Road*,
a Pura Belpré Honor Book, also written by
Alexandra Diaz.

★ "An important, must-have addition to the growing
body of literature with immigrant themes."
—*School Library Journal* (starred review)

From the kitchen came a piercing scream. The green colored pencil slipped, streaking across the almost-finished portrait of a lizard Jaime Rivera had been working on for the last half hour. As he jumped to his feet, a wave of dizziness hit him, leftover from the fever that had kept him home from school that morning. It took a second for his vision to clear, his hand braced on the sill of the glassless window that no longer held the posing lizard. He took a deep breath before bursting into the kitchen. The wailing only grew louder.

No, no, no, no, please no, he thought. It couldn't be, couldn't. It had to be something else. *Please!*

"*¿Qué . . .*" Jaime stopped short. Mamá was slumped on the plastic table, crying into her arms. Papá stood behind her with a hand on her back. Despite his quiet stance, his broad shoulders were hunched, making him look as distraught as Mamá.

At the sound of Jaime's entrance, Mamá looked up. Streaks of black, brown, and tan covered her normally perfectly made-up face. She beckoned him closer, pulled him onto her lap, and held him as if he were two instead of twelve. Papá's strong arms encircled both of them.

For a second Jaime allowed himself to melt into his parents' embrace. But only for a second. Dread twisted his stomach into a knot. *It* had happened, something he'd feared for a long time. He had convinced himself with all his might that it wouldn't, couldn't happen, because he didn't have anything to offer *them*. But *they* obviously disagreed. *They* had made that clear two weeks ago. If only he were wrong, and it wasn't that at all.

The incident that had happened two weeks ago came back to him; his former friend Pulguita had called over Jaime and his cousin Miguel as they were walking home from school.

"What does he want?" Jaime had muttered under his breath.

"I don't know. But at least he's alone." Miguel looked up and down the dirt street before crossing it. Jaime doublechecked as well. Good. *They* weren't around.

Miguel stopped a few meters away from the boy.

Jaime folded his arms across his chest, keeping more distance between himself and his former friend.

Pulguita leaned against a deteriorating cinder-block wall. His slicked-back black hair gave him the look of a little boy pretending to be his papá. Fourteen and unlikely to grow anymore, Pulguita was still a head shorter than Jaime and Miguel, who were two years younger. But his height wasn't the only reason he went by the name that meant "little flea."

"¿Qué?" Miguel asked, barely opening his mouth.

Pulguita threw his hands in the air as if he didn't understand the hostility and laughed. Even at Jaime's distance he caught a whiff of cigarette and alcohol breath. "Can't a boy say hi to his old friends?"

"No," both Miguel and Jaime answered. Not when the boy was Pulguita. Not when he had become one of *them*.

Until last year, Jaime and Miguel had played with the tiny, dirty boy. Then things started going missing—first bananas from the backyard and tortillas wrapped in a dish towel; later new shoes and Jaime's drawing charcoals that had been a birthday present. Jaime and Miguel had stopped inviting Pulguita to their houses, and the little flea had found new "friends."

Now Pulguita's clothes were immaculate. From his white sleeveless undershirt and blue *fútbol* shorts to his white socks stretched tight to his calves and white Nike high-tops, everything he had on was new and expensive. To prove it, he pulled out his flashy iPhone and twirled it around his palm, making sure the cousins noticed. Oh, Jaime noticed it. The only phone anyone in his family could afford belonged to Tío Daniel, Miguel's papá. He shared it with Jaime's family and other relatives, but there was nothing fancy or smart about it, just one of those old flip ones.

Pulguita turned to Jaime with a sly grin. "I saw your *mami* the other day, carrying a heavy laundry basket. Looks like that leg is still bothering her."

"You leave Tía out of this." Miguel took a step closer, his eyes glaring at him. Pulguita ignored the threat as he continued showing off the fancy phone.

"Sure would be nice, wouldn't it, if she didn't have to work so hard. If she could relax in front of *la tele* with her leg up. You two were always nice to me. I'd like to help you out, you know."

"We don't need your help," Jaime said, but in the back of his mind he was intrigued. Mamá had been a teenager when she had broken her leg and it had been set incorrectly. Her limp was barely noticeable when she walked, but the injury kept her from jobs that required standing or sitting all day. She earned next to nothing washing and ironing clothes for rich ladies. Papá made barely enough at the chocolate plantation to keep them fed and sheltered in their small house that consisted of two small rooms: a sleeping one and a kitchen. The outhouse was, well, outside.

If they had extra money, just a tiny bit more, maybe his parents wouldn't need to work so hard. Maybe they could live better. But not by earning money the way Pulguita offered. It wouldn't be worth it.

Right?

Pulguita's smile widened as if he were mocking them. "You'll change your mind. Someday you'll want our help."

Our help. The words pounded repeatedly in Jaime's head. His stomach twisted at the thought of what Pulguita and his new friends expected in exchange for *help*.

"Not until your farts smell like jasmine," Miguel assured him. Jaime nodded. He couldn't do anything else.

With a shrug Pulguita tapped a code on his phone before bringing it to his ear, stuffed the other hand deep into his pocket, and swaggered away.

Jaime had tried to put the confrontation with Pulguita out of his mind. Until now, in the kitchen, with his mamá wailing and both of his parents smothering him.

Something was wrong. Horribly wrong. And he had a feeling he knew what.

His body tensed up to break free, but Mamá's grip only got tighter.

"*Ay Jaime, mi ángel,*" she said between her cries. "What would I do without you?"

Mamá released him. Her dark eyes were puffy and red. Her black wavy hair hung in tangled, wet clumps around her face. Jaime brushed a strand away from her eyes, something she used to do for him when he was younger and feeling upset.

She took two deep breaths and stared into Jaime's brown eyes. "It's Miguel."

Jaime scrambled out of his mamá's lap. Papá reached out for him, but he jerked away. The dizziness that had almost overcome Jaime in the bedroom threatened to overtake him again.

Miguel just has the flu, Jaime tried to convince himself. After all, Jaime had been pretty feverish this morning too. *That's it. Just a bad flu.*

But that didn't explain Mamá's crying, why she looked at him like it would be the last time.

"What's happened?" The words choked him.

Mamá averted her makeup-streaked red eyes. "He's dead."

"No." Because even though he had guessed the possibility, it couldn't be true. Not Miguel. Not his brave cousin. Not his best friend.

"He was walking through Parque de San José after school. And . . ." Mamá took a deep breath. "The Alphas surrounded him."

Of course, *them.* Jaime wrapped his arms tightly around himself, desperate to stop the shaking that had taken over his body. His sore throat from this morning made it impossible to swallow or breathe. Parque de San José. He and Miguel cut across the small park every day, twice a day, on their way to school and back. At night it was filled with drunks and druggies, but during the day, with everyone else who walked through it, it had always felt safe enough.

Had. Not anymore.

"Di—did they—how—*¿qué?*" Jaime stumbled over the words. His mind had gone blurry.

A fresh wave of tears overtook Mamá. When she couldn't answer, Papá said the words she couldn't. "Six or seven gang members approached him. Including Pulguita."

Jaime cringed. Of course, Pulguita. If this was the puny, stinking pest's idea of "helping" . . .

Papá pressed his fingers against the bridge of his prominent nose before he continued, "Hermán Domingo was walking by. He saw everything. The Alphas told Miguel he'd be an asset to the gang and should join them. Miguel told them to leave him alone. That's when they started hitting him."

"Stop." Jaime didn't want to know more. He could see the Alpha gang members in his head—some big and burly, some lean and quick, and Pulguita, small enough to be squashed. All of them punching and kicking until Miguel fell to the ground. If only Jaime had been there.

"There was no stopping them," Papá said as if he'd read

Jaime's mind. "If Hermán or anyone had interfered, they would have put a bullet in his head. Like they did to José Adolfo Torres, Santiago Ruís, Lo—"

Jaime stopped listening because he knew the names. Older boys he'd gone to school with, grown men with wives and children. People who tried to stand up to the violent gang; people who were now dead.

Dead, *muerto*. Like Miguel. His cousin had come over that morning. His face, with its lopsided smile, ecstatic over his scholarship into the exclusive science *prevocacional* school in the city twenty kilometers away: he had always wanted to be an engineer. His disappointment that Jaime was sick and couldn't walk to school with him disappeared as Miguel counted all the people he had to tell his good news to.

Guilt blazed in Jaime's chest as he gasped for air. Why Miguel? Why not him? The room suddenly didn't seem to have enough of it even with the humid breeze coming in from the glassless windows. His fault.

The gang had a strong presence in their small Guatemalan village and other villages in the area. Kids younger than Jaime were addicted to the cocaine the Alphas supplied. Shopkeepers were "asked" to pay the Alphas for protection: the protection they offered was from themselves. Protection from being robbed, or killed, if refused.

Miguel.

Jaime crouched down on the bare dirt floor, hiding his face in his arms. If only he hadn't been sick this morning. If he had walked through the park with Miguel like always, could he have stopped them from attacking? Two against six was better than one against six. Except Jaime had never been good at fighting. Would it have been easier to give in? Become the gang's newest member? Sell drugs on street corners, demand "insurance" from villagers, kill anyone who refused or got in his way? No, he couldn't have done things like that, but he wouldn't have been able to stand up to the Alphas either.

He'd never been brave like his cousin.

"Here," Mamá's voice said softly. Jaime looked up from his crumpled spot on the floor. Mamá had put the coffee on the stove and cleaned herself up. Her eyes were still red, but now she just looked tired, and old. She offered him sweet and milky *café con leche*. Like it would help.

Still, he held the cup, wrapping his hands around the ceramic mug as if it were a cold day instead of a suffocating one. He took a deep breath; after all, he'd been with Miguel that day when Pulguita had made his "offer."

"Will I be next?"

His parents didn't look at him. Mamá started crying again and Papá shook his head. Jaime got his answer.

"I don't want to die. But I don't want to kill people either. What can I do?" he asked the coffee cup in his hands, like a fortune-telling *bruja* might do with tea leaves. Neither the coffee, nor his parents, answered him.

There was nothing he could do. No one escaped the Alphas.